To all my cats, past, present and future, and my father: I affectionately dedicate this book.

CW01498959

CHAPTER ONE

Three o'clock on New Year's Eve and the first vestiges of dusk apparent in the leaden skies. All day long, rain had threatened from the west but the storm clouds had stayed huddled in the corner of the horizon and the wind had held them at bay. Habitation here in this desolate northern region was sparse and many abandoned houses were slowly sliding into decay. Roofs were eaten away as slate after slate crumbled and fell, losing themselves in the wiry moorland grass. The sheep, sole residents of the remote paths, ate round them and, in time, consumed the dust and fragments of their shape.

The turnpike road to the village of Scar's End was a lonely place on this winter afternoon and the few bedraggled cottages, spasmodically scattered over the leeward end of the habitation, had yet to light their candles and draw their shutters. The century was the nineteenth and nearly half way through, with 1849 being about to draw breath in a few hours. The church clock continued to beat out the passage of the declining year and deemed itself important enough to govern the transition of the old to the new. Had it not rung the hour and the half hour for more than a century without man's intervention? Besides, who, apart from the pastor and those bending the knee in worship, ever lifted their eyes upwards to gaze critically or otherwise at his ornate face? Over time, some of this ornateness had found its way to the church yard beneath but money was in short supply and, as long as the old timekeeper ticked his way through the day, no-one intended to restore him to his former glory. He rang now, loud and clear, three resounding chimes that flew over the surrounding moorlands and cared not a wit that he was behind the doctor's watch or the inn's golden clock.

Just after the timekeeper had ceased his ministrations, the sound of wheels broke the pervading dusk and an untidy phaeton broke upon the scene, the driver whipping the exhausted horse as he gazed anxiously around him. Dusk in this region was terrifying and he had no desire to remain

Whittle's Vampires

Emily Starr

Published in 2020 by FeedARead.com Publishing

A CIP catalogue record for this title is available from the
British Library.

Also by the same author:

Westerdale (unavailable)
Rainharrow (unavailable)
Heaton
The Calling
Bleak Spirit (about the Brontes)
Split Moonbeam (the story of my great-grandmother)
Summer Madness
The Awakening
Winter Violet
Gabriel Messenger
Briarly

here one second longer than necessary. The sharp clatter of hooves brought a few to their windows but otherwise the coach passed through unnoticed and sought the turnpike road, up over the shoulder of the nearby crag and out onto the open moor. After a while, another road presented itself and this the driver took, having to check his speed as the path narrowed and twisted and turned almost back on itself. He uttered a curse but the wind whipped the words from his frozen lips and presently, a house came into view to which the carriage hastened.

It was an ugly, sprawling dwelling, built during the last century and added to as various buyers came and went, each with their own idea of architecture but nothing about it could be said to be pleasing to the eye and the last inhabitant had pronounced it serviceable to his desire for seclusion. Finding religion in later life, he had piled his books against the doorways and lived the existence of a hermit, scarcely opening his door and never being seen in the village. Thus had he died – alone and isolated, so the locals pronounced that it was a good job it was a cold summer or the man would have rotted.

The phaeton reached the door and the driver jumped down, holding the restive horse who, now he had stopped, was anxious to be away again, exhausted or not. The man opened the carriage door and cried,

"The beast desires to go and so do I. Make haste and hold the horse so I may unload your trunk and thus, get on my way."

The addressed individual stirred within the vehicle and, after a struggle, came forth, tightening her bonnet as the wind rose to assail her. She held the horse's head and watched as her luggage was thrown down.

"What is it about this place that terrifies you so, Mr Clowton? Surely you desire to refresh yourself before the long journey back?"

"In there, madam? I think not."

"But I have hired a servant to live there and..."

"Yes, Miss Whittle – perhaps so for now but how many will stay? Old Mr Whittle could find no help when he first went there and had to make do alone, even before the religion conquered him."

"My uncle was incessantly mean, Mr Clowton and refused to pay a decent wage, whereas I almost doubled it to secure help."

"Treble the wage would not entice me to step foot over the threshold, miss!"

"Then let us be grateful that the maid I hired has gone ahead of us and seemingly lit and warmed the place. Will you not take some tea before you leave?"

"Not a drop, miss, not a drop. Not a crumb of victuals nor a splash of liquid."

"What if I bring you some out, for I know the horse requires water and you too must take refreshment?"

The carrier saw sense in this but he still refused to approach the door and, if anything, drew back now the luggage was unloaded.

"A bucket of water then, for the nag, but anything out of there would either be poisoned or cursed, miss!"

"Very well then, refreshment for the horse and nothing for you."

She rang the bell loudly and the carrier shuddered. Footsteps could be heard from within and presently, a short, fresh-faced girl answered and bade her mistress come in.

"My luggage," replied Miss Whittle, "I will help you since the driver refuses entry and only wants some water for his horse before setting off. You are far younger than I thought."

"Nineteen last birthday, miss, and fit and strong."

The two women pulled and pushed the trunk into the hallway and Miss Whittle had the first view of her inheritance, which was hardly conducive to joy. She wrinkled her nose at the smell of damp.

"Do you have a bucket?" she said now.

"Yes Miss."

"Then fill it with water for the horse and give this to the carrier," and she then handed over some money to the maid,

"And see if the man will come in with you asking him, for he'll not stir for me!"

The young girl departed to carry out her orders, and the owner of this crumbling mansion wandered round the lofty hall with a worried expression on her face.

Looking up at the ceilings brought no relief and, as she wandered from room to room – those that were open at the moment anyway, her worst fears were confirmed. Her uncle had clearly done nothing in his twelve year occupation of the property. Peeling wallpaper, large, irregular patches of damp and green mould all greeted her gaze and she decided not to inspect any further but hurried downstairs to the kitchen. Here, at least, a huge fire blazed and she warmed her cold hands by it.   The maid was nowhere to be seen but a kettle was singing on the blaze and something smelling like tea darkened a white vessel on the table. Verity, for so had she been christened, found a cloth and poured the silver stream onto the fragrant leaves. Just as she did so, her maid entered and she heard the departing sound of hooves.

"He refused all victuals or beverages, miss and once the horse had supped, he was eager to be away. Happen he has more work on."

"Not tonight, Liddy, but he has come many miles out of his way and it seems, even though he is a stranger, he has heard odd reports of this house or the village."

Liddy turned away at this and concealed a frown. She was anxious to continue in her position but she knew, in time, the truth would come out. When she turned to her mistress, she was more composed.

"Your uncle was a recluse and no-one came here, miss. Tales are bound to have been created around the myth of a hermit and his desire for seclusion. Religion or not, it was not right...well, not conducive to the man's sanity and some said he went mad from isolation. No-one called, and he even left his penny for bread under a rock near the gate and would only collect the loaf under cover of darkness."

"But what possessed him to take the vow of silence? I well remember him in my youth as a gregarious man, pleased by any company and who took a delight in conversation."

"Some said it was the secrets of the house that silenced him, miss, and some said it was the village. They are an odd lot here and that is understating it. I doubt you will be received with kindness."

"Since I have no other place to go, Liddy, I must just bear that as I can. Are they actively hostile then to outsiders?"

"Not actively, miss, but you will be received with great suspicion and wariness, especially seeing who your relation was and your sex."

"It seems I hear it already, 'A woman, and a young, unmarried one at that, residing in that house! What can she mean by it?' Maybe they will call out of curiosity?"

Liddy shook her head. She had only painted half a picture but she felt she had said enough and shrugged the question off.

"Doubtless you are self-sufficient in your mind, miss, and you have me to talk to but do not think of a sweetheart here, as the men are gruff and unyielding."

"I was thinking of no such thing, Liddy. 'Romance'...'Love'...these are not words to trip off my tongue after what I have been through. Losing both my parents so close together, then my only sister, then my brother killed in a duel over the hand of a woman. Huh, a hussy I should say, toying with his affections and then marrying the victor - who she declared she hated - until she found him wealthy!"

"A sorry tale, miss, sorry indeed. And now you have come here and are facing the biggest challenge of your life so far! Have you seen the state of the rooms upstairs?"

"Yes, sadly. You said you managed to turn two into chambers for us, of a sort, but I could not find them in my travels."

"I locked them up, miss. Things are strange round about and I felt safer that they were behind a key. I will show you

8

now," So saying, she took two keys from a hook above the fire and saw the tea had been made.

"A cup first, miss?" she asked.

"Yes, Liddy, mash it for strength, as I believe they do here, for I am thirsty."

"And food? I have some bread and little cakes made earlier on the griddle?"

"Just tea for now and maybe a meal later, if you have anything in?"

"Yes, miss, for there was food still growing in the garden. For all his seclusion from society, your uncle grew many crops and folk often spotted him cultivating potatoes or wheat or barley. He often made his own bread and oatcakes too and some said the finest for miles around although, of course, few tasted them. But the tramps that came knocking were sometimes sent away with one as thick as a doorstep and a meal for any man! I found potatoes and winter vegetables in profusion, as your uncle ate no meat and pronounced it poison from the Devil."

"My mother ate no meat either, Liddy - them being raised together as it were - and it has not been part of my diet for many a year. I am content with vegetables and bread."

"Seemingly that is why you are so small, miss, but yes, I will cook some of the vegetables later. They are particularly fine and huge in size, great carrots, cabbages and clean white potatoes. There was talk of what he used to grow them but no-one knew. He sold some in the village, well he never came of course but he sent a boy to collect the pennies."

They had finished their tea and whilst Verity drained a second cup, Liddy washed up the vessels and made up the fire. She filled a warming pan from the fire and then the two women ascended with the keys. The rank smell of mould greeted them but Verity was beginning to get used to it and as her uncle had left but thirty pounds, she knew that would never be enough to renovate the place.

"And they call it Coombe Heights around here do they, Liddy?"

"Yes, miss, amongst other things."

9

"Such as?"

"Well, when your uncle lived here, it was always referred to as 'The Mad House'..."

"I wonder how they will talk of it now that I am here?"

"Not favourably, miss, I think."

They had reached the upper floor and Liddy led the way to the end of the corridor, where two rooms faced each other with an ivy covered window between, refusing to let in even a vestige of light. It was dark now and past four o'clock and both midnight and the New Year were fast approaching.

The maid opened the first door.

"Your room, miss, and the bigger of the two of course. I am just across the corridor should you feel lonely. This place can instil fear in even the bravest at times. My father came up here from time to time and was never easy, for he felt he could not eat or drink and the air oppressive with he knew not what. Many have felt it, I know."

"And do you feel it too?" asked Verity, "Will you stay or go like I understand other servants have before my uncle's time?"

"I'll stay, miss, as I need the money and besides, I don't believe all I hear."

"So you have heard more?"

"Mere rumours and fancy tales, spread by men with too much time on their hands and too much imagination. Stories get embroidered as they are passed on and each mouth adds a different sentence. Why, by the time fifty have talked about it the entire subject has altered!"

Verity picked up on the girl's tone. She sounded like she did not believe what she preached.

"I suppose time will prove if any of these tales have any foundation in fact," she replied now, gazing round at her room with a modicum of approval.

The bed was duly turned and the warming pan put in, and Verity was pleased to see new curtains at the window, as most rooms contained what she could only describe as rags.

"My uncle had a morbid fear of fire, so most of the rooms were furnished with shutters and blinds but his money ran out when it came to the upstairs," Verity told her maid.

There was an old but serviceable wardrobe, a set of drawers, a ewer and basin and a large trunk which proved to be empty when Verity looked in. As it bore nautical themes, she concluded it must have belonged to her uncle, who was a seafaring man in his younger days.

"You have done well, Liddy," she concluded, "This room is perfectly fit for habitation and I hope yours is the same."

"It is very tolerable, miss but just not so big. I am well content with it."

"Good. Then all that remains is for me to decide what to do with my inheritance. Should I sell it, would you say?"

Liddy gave a short laugh.

"I think you would find that hard, miss," she replied, "Whenever this came up for sale, why, it was years before someone took it and even then, they rarely stayed long."

"Apart from my uncle, who saw it as a fitting place to end his life."

"I think he cleaved to the land, miss. The soil is very rich hereabouts for growing, so your uncle – God rest his soul – discovered he could more or less be self-sufficient, apart from years when the weather played havoc with his crops."

"And is it wild here then, Liddy, even in the summer?"

"It can be, miss, but then again, it can be gentle, with plenty of rain to bring forth the grain. I think in my years I have seen more famine than feast but even so, I think it is worth me trying to cultivate our food, especially as vegetables are happily growing already."

"Well, it is but a couple of months since my uncle's untimely death and as he never expected it, he obviously saw the garden was well stocked for the winter. They are still not sure what he died of. The doctor was never called until a tramp, knocking at the door for food, saw a lifeless body propped up by the window. God knows how long he had been dead. Even then, the medic found his organs all intact but his system bloodless and low. Anaemia, I think he called it. What do you think could have caused that, Liddy?"

The girl looked uncomfortable.

"Not being a medical person, I could not say, miss. He was over eighty, was he not?"

"Seventy-four."

"Old age and perhaps a modicum of insanity from the isolation which had resulted in self-neglect?"

"But a man who stocked his garden for the coming winter and then died with most of the produce still in the soil?"

"It shows that he did not expect it, miss, but then when the Grim Reaper knocks at the door demanding admission, few can refuse him, however much they want to stay and munch on their homegrown parsnips at Christmas!"

Several hours later, Verity stood at the window of her room, having decided not to stay up and see in the New Year. For one thing, she was exhausted and for another, there was only Liddy to keep her company and the girl was already getting ideas way above her station. Verity, who had been used to keeping servants at arms' length, felt the girl ran on too much and there was definitely no 'speaking when spoken to' – Liddy was happy to interrupt and even challenge Verity's views. Still, it was her first position away from home and the age difference was not great.

She heard a slight noise at the window and drew back the curtain to look. A bat! A bat fluttering at the pane as though seeking admission. She watched in horror as the creature continued its assault on the window and then, seemingly exhausted, it flew off into the darkness.

Verity dropped the curtain. Now why would such a creature of the open skies seek shelter within a house? There were no insects here for it to prey upon. She picked up the curtain and looked again. Yes! There was the very same creature, crawling up the outside of the building! She gave a shudder. And there was another!

"Liddy! Liddy!"

The girl seemed to be asleep and banging at her chamber door brought no response but bats, behaving almost like humans in seeking shelter from the cold of New Year? How could that be happening?

She returned to the window but all sight of them had vanished. Did she dream it? Was she so tired that her thoughts had betrayed her and slipped her into an illusion for a moment?

She got ready for bed, unpacking her trunk for her night wear and hanging the other clothes in the dark wardrobe, although it smelt of must and decay and she was afraid the same odour would be transferred to her precious gowns. Why did everything here seem to be in a perpetual state of decay? And would she herself be taken over by this after she had resided here for a few weeks?

"I think I must sell it, no matter how long it takes," she said aloud, "This is no place for me."

The bed was warm and although she could hear strange noises outside, she put it down to the nocturnal animals coming out to hunt. The creatures of the night and what music they make!

The day had been long and so many pictures flashed before her eyes. She felt exhausted by what had been achieved so far; such a massive change.

She slept.

CHAPTER TWO

She awoke with a sense of being disturbed. Nothing moved in the room and the darkness was universal. Dimly, in the distance, the chimes of the church clock rang out. Twelve. She counted them slowly under her breath. A New Year. Yet she had hardly slept.

She struggled up and the cold bit her. Tap, tap, tap. Just like fingernails on glass. Somehow, intuition told her it was the bats returning but she felt she had to see them and they were drawing her into their tangled web, although her soul recoiled from the horror of their furry bodies and tiny, red eyes.

Moving as though in a dream, she pulled the curtain back and the moonlight hit her. "Fresh blood," Their malevolent eyes were upon her and the wall opposite the window was thick with them. They crowded the brickwork, waiting for a space on the window to try their luck. The pane rattled with their vibrating bodies.
"Blood! Blood!"

She pulled the curtains shut and made for the door.
"Liddy! Liddy!" she called. No answer but by persistently banging on the door, she finally got a reaction.

Liddy appeared in cap and gown, her long hair done up in a plait that trailed down her back.
"Miss?" Her voice offered a safe harbour in a sea of darkness, "Wait – I'll get a candle."

She bustled away leaving Verity in the eldritch blackness of midnight. Still the tap, tap, tap of the creatures' wings reached Verity's ears and their voices cried,
"Fresh blood! Fresh blood!"
"Hurry up, Liddy," she shouted. Anything to try and cover the noise of their assault. "Quick! They are trying to gain admittance!"

Liddy came flying up the stairs with a light.
"Who is, miss?" she asked.

Verity held up a finger. She turned her head to the door of her room. The noises had stopped. Verity ran into the chamber and bade her maid follow.

"In here quickly, Liddy, and bring that candle!"

She strode to the window and, taking a deep breath, she pulled back the curtain. The window and house front were empty. Not a single bat, not a single beat of those scaly wings...

"What was it, miss?" asked Liddy, raising the light to her mistress's pale face, "What did you see?"

"Hundreds and hundreds of bats crawling over the stonework, knocking at the glass, trying to gain entrance!" It sounded ridiculous. Who said there were hundreds? She had not counted them. Maybe hundreds was an exaggeration.

"Fifty...yes, fifty or so and maybe more," her voice trailed away as the shock hit her. Was that a flutter of bony wings deep in the darkness?

She flung herself at the window and struggled vainly to free it. Liddy, however, stopped her and pulled her hands off.

"Miss, you mustn't!"

Verity was surprised at the force of her maid's intervention and she moved away.

"What is happening here, Liddy? Do you know? Why did you stop me opening the window?"

"It - it - is cold, miss, and very dark."

"But those creatures! I mean, I have seen bats before but not that size! And why do they seek entry to the world of man? What here would attract them? And that cry, 'Fresh blood fresh blood,' What does that mean?"

"I...I don't know, miss."

"And you have heard no tales involving bats pertaining to this house?"

"One always hears tales, miss, about an empty house, but no, never concerning bats."

Verity was perplexed but there seemed nothing for it but to return to bed. It seemed Liddy had said her piece and no more information was going to come from her lips. Either she was as genuinely confused as her mistress or she had her own reasons for remaining silent.

"Do you need me any further tonight, miss?" she said now, avoiding Verity's eyes.

Her mistress woke from her far from sanguine reflections and shook her head.

"No, you go back to bed. I will see you in the morning."

"And after a few hours of oblivion, will you feel you dreamt it, miss? The bats, I mean."

Again, Verity shook her head and her dark, luxuriant hair cascaded over her face. She gazed at the window, now spattered by driving rain.

"If I slept for a hundred years, Liddy, I would still wake to recognise it as reality."

Liddy did not reply but took the candle and vanished into the darkness, and Verity was once more alone. Half an hour into a New Year and high drama already, she thought.

She returned to bed but for a long while sleep eluded her. She was cold, then hot, then every nocturnal noise the house made alerted her senses, just when she was praying they would calm. The window, however, remained silent now the rain had passed over them.

'And these creatures,' pondered her primeval brain, 'What dark world did they come from and had they now returned to it? Would they repeat their frenzy, as soon as black graced the skies and turned them inky? Perhaps I did indeed dream them,' said her logical brain calmly, 'Or maybe they are a species of bat known only to the local area. Perhaps people in the village had seen them and could shed some light on their appearance.'

One o'clock rang out and still she remained wakeful. Then the wind got up and flung hailstones at the window bringing back sharp pictures, so she thought for a minute the bats had returned. The last thing she heard was the rattle of the ill-fitting catch and then, thankfully, sleep engulfed her.

It was broad daylight when she awoke and sounds from downstairs told her Liddy was already up and working. She lay there luxuriating in the fact that she was, indeed, mistress of this establishment and, as such, had no longer to do menial work. She looked at her hands which were white and unblemished but, oh, how sore they had been last year when she had laboured to earn a crust for her sick parents. Alas, both had sought the peace of the grave and now, her uncle with them. Were they all safe together in heaven or was there, as some thought, only the numbing blackness to come when you quit this world? And, if so, where did creatures come from like those last night? Had they once inhabited a bright world like this, and was it their wickedness that sent them into the bodies of bats? Would they appear again tonight and had they appeared every night for the past few centuries trying in vain to gain admittance?

She found an ancient bell beside her bed on the old cabinet and rang it now. Would Liddy be offended by its use, she wondered casually? Steps were heard on the stairs and a knock at the door.

"Come in!" called Verity sitting up in bed, "Good morning, Liddy, have you lit the fires and can you bring me up hot water for my toilet?"

"Yes, miss, of course and I shall start breakfast too, it wanting only two minutes to 9 o'clock."

"Really? I could not believe I slept so late."

"It is no matter, miss. No work to attend to and the village so quiet this New Year's Day."

"You have been out already then?"

"Yes, miss. Just to the mill and back."

"I had a thought to ask them if they knew anything of the bats..."

"I wouldn't, miss. They still label this house as the retreat of madness. Best lead by example. Show them you are a determined woman of business."

"But I am not, Liddy. I have inherited a pile of crumbling bricks and barely have the money to put it to rights and then, how shall I live?"

"By the sweat of your brow if you have to, miss. You have an intelligent look about you that will never leave you short of money, I know."

"Well you have more faith in me than I have in myself, I must say. Yes, I can pay your wages for a year or so but that may be all, so then where will you go?"

"I shall advertise, miss, when you no longer require my services and I shall beg you for a good reference when the time comes. I hope I will have served you faithfully by then."

"Well, time marches on, Liddy, so please do my bidding, and let us hope neither of us becomes penniless or without a place to lay our heads."

Half an hour later, Verity was breakfasting in the cold splendour of the living room, which remained icy despite the leaping flames of the fire. This is an austere house, she thought,6 as she drank her tea. Studying the high ceilings and huge panes of murky glass that made up the windows, she was not surprised. None of the pieces of glass quite fitted and the gaps were evident, so that draughts prevailed and the air was chill. Only right next to the fire did any heat reign and Verity warmed her hands now and called to Liddy to take out the breakfast tray.

What direction will my life take from here, she wondered? Am I doomed to remain and stagnate within these walls, since opinion seems to state that the house will not sell easily?

"I am not sure it offers any life for me," she mused aloud.

Scarcely had these words escaped her mouth, when she heard a loud banging upon the front door and hastening to the window, she remained hidden in the shadow of the blinds whilst spying on the caller. A tall, well-built man, with his features obscured by a large hat, stood there. He carried a silver topped cane and, when no answer was apparent to his knock, he tapped with it several times and gave an impatient sigh.

Where was Liddy, Verity wondered and was it seemly to answer the door herself, seeing as her maid did not appear to

18

be vigilant? Just then she heard a noise in the kitchen and rapid steps in the hall approaching the front door, which was then swung open.

"Sorry, sir, sorry, I was picking fresh herbs in the garden and Mistress has only lately moved in..."

"So I understand," Verity heard the man announce in rather gruff tones. He clipped his words rather too fine for a local but she could not place his accent. A Londoner?

"Can I speak with your Mistress?" he asked now.

It seemed Liddy was rather confused about her answer and course of action, so Verity felt there was nothing else to do but step into the hallway. This she duly did, shyness not being a natural part of her character and besides, this fine-looking gentleman intrigued her; she was very young after all.

She found Liddy twisting a cloth round and round in her hands, whilst a quantity of green foliage fell, crushed, to the floor.

"Tell the gentleman I will see him," she told Liddy, "And please clear that vegetation up, Liddy, as it will not be fit for consumption now, even with rigorous washing." She bowed her head to the man who touched his top hat in acknowledgement.

Verity then withdrew into the front room and the gentleman soon followed, having been stripped of his hat, cane and greatcoat.

"A cold day, Miss er..." he began, warming his hands by the fire.

"Whittle."

"Ah," a little light crept into his face.

"Then Mr Whittle, lately deceased, is..."

"My uncle. My father's brother to be precise."

"And he had no one else to leave the property to then?"

"Not a soul as far as I understand but you probably know better than I do how he lived, sir. Hand to mouth. Well, he left a few pounds, hence the servant but precious little to do up this mouldering, old pile!"

The gentleman nodded.

"And do you intend to do that, Miss Whittle? Do you intend to repair this great, desolate house and live here?"

This was a bit too intrusive for Verity's liking and her hackles were up as she said,

"And if I do Mr er...? If I do, what business is it of yours, may I ask?"

The gentleman acknowledged her angry words.

"I am sorry, I have run on far too fast, as usual. My anxiety for your safety has killed any civility in my tone. I am Mr Pyne, lately come to this place, only a few weeks before your uncle died."

Verity accepted this apology but remained intrigued.

"So why did you come?" she asked now.

The gentleman looked a shade awkward.

"I was called," he replied, "I was summoned by the locals to investigate what was occurring within the walls of this house," and as he said those words, he gazed round the cold, lofty room.

Verity was confused.

"And did you find any answers?" she continued, gazing at him with huge eyes, "I mean, did my uncle let you in or even talk to you?"

"He did not. So I had to observe him from afar, as it were, for I was determined to find out what was happening here. And what I saw, Miss Whittle, instilled the fear of God in me!"

He said this with such vehemence that Verity felt the force of his words reverberating around the room. It sounded like the house was echoing his words, so long did they ring in the chilly air.

"So what was it, Mr Pyne, that took your breath away and had you begging God for protection?"

"There is no easy way to say this, Miss Whittle, but I believe your uncle was involved with vampires!"

Verity gasped. Illegal whisky, stolen tobacco and burgled goods she could believe of her uncle but vampires? A creature that only existed in the imagination of the most fevered or in Gothic legends?

She found herself grinning suddenly. Surely Mr Pyne was jesting with her?

Seeing her relax into amusement, the gentleman stepped forth and assured her it was no laughing matter.

"I beseech you, Miss Whittle, do not even consider this place as a suitable home for such as your good self! My findings were sketchy, I'll own."

"So nothing concrete?"

"Well, it seems your uncle may not even be dead. Folk have seen him since that was declared as his demise."

"He's…he's not dead?"

"Part of the Undead it seems. Those doomed never to die but to wander the earth in whatever form their master dictates, and that changes frequently of course, on the trail of blood. Fresh blood."

His words made Verity wince. Fresh blood. Exactly what the voices of the bats were calling to her but why should she, a mere mortal, be able to hear them so clearly?

"Tell me, Mr Pyne, could they...would they...wander our world as bats? Those loathsome, furry creatures that fly by night and seek to tangle themselves in our hair?"

The gentleman was so taken aback by her question that he could not frame an answer. Verity repeated her question and searched his face for clues as to what he was thinking. Was this some vast jest that as a newcomer she was forced to be part of, like some weird village ritual?

"Very possibly, miss, very possibly," he said at last but his voice trailed away.

He stood for a minute or two to recover himself as her words had hit him hard.

"You have seen something, so it is as I feared, one night here and they have tried to make contact with you."

"Who has?"

She was trying to divert his attention away from what she had witnessed and force him to reveal further knowledge, so she could judge whether this whole thing was a prank played upon a newcomer.

"Tell me what you saw," he replied, ignoring her question. He sounded desperate and he moved a few steps closer to her so that Verity felt a bit threatened; she hardly knew this man after all.

"You are forgetting your manners, Mr Pyne," she said, taking a step away from him.

"Forgive me, Miss Whittle, but this is, I assure you, nothing to be taken lightly or in a jovial manner."

"Are you sure? Not a prank you have invented to entertain a newcomer and make her think she has inherited a madhouse?"

"I am afraid you may have done that anyway, Miss Whittle, but I doubt anyone will be suffused with mirth when the true secret of the place is revealed!"

"And you expect that to happen, do you?"

"With your assistance, yes, I do. Your uncle blocked me at every turn but I am hoping you will be more pliable."

"And put myself in danger, you mean."

"Miss Whittle, you were in danger the minute you walked into this building and claimed it as your own. With responsibility like this comes grave danger. You have inherited an eternal mystery."

"But seeing how little you know, can you really be sure of that?"

"Then please, tell me what you saw. Why would you suddenly ask a question like that about bats? Do you know much about vampires?"

"Not a thing, Mr Pyne, I assure you."

"So what have you seen? Tell me and then I can add it to my scant file of knowledge gleaned about this house. We can add pieces to the pictures and we can solve this between the two of us."

"No, Mr Pyne, you tell me your findings first and I will judge whether I will reveal my secret, as I call it."

"Very well. But it may take an hour or two, I warn you, so shall we both be seated? It may shock you and it will certainly worry you."

"I shall be the judge of that, Mr Pyne. I may view your story as a total fabrication and then my secret will go to the grave with me."

"Do not use such words, Miss Whittle, for I fear they may indeed, come true."

"I have no plans whatsoever for today, sir, and no business to attend to, so I am very happy to give you an audience."

Verity put fuel on the fire and they both sat.

"I am no ragamuffin or fly-by-night, Miss Whittle, as hopefully you can see from my dress. My father was a gentleman and one of business too, carving letters on rich men's tombstones and he thought I would do the same. But the gift was lacking in me or perhaps it was the application, I don't know, and so I found myself at a desk, as an under-clerk in an export office in London.

Desiring to better myself with education, I applied to a college of learning and that, Miss Whittle, is where I met my first vampire."

He said the word as he would have done 'doctor' or 'undertaker'– in a very matter-of-fact tone that struck Verity with a shiver of fear. She stirred in her chair and looked incredulous.

"Oh, he was a vampire alright," continued the speaker, "No wings or red eyes but the never-ending lust for blood, and room-mate after room-mate found stiff and bloodless after complaining of weird dreams, all with the tell-tale puncture wounds in the neck and the smile of the Devil on their face. Oh, they taught me a lot at that university of life, and they opened my eyes to the fact that such creatures are all around us. I knew the signs, I could spot the clues and my life changed from that moment. I looked at everyone differently. I could not un-know, as it were, and it made me vigilant.

"After I had finished my studies, I set myself up in business as an architect but that was really a cover...a sham. Yes, I had the qualifications to design, and I did but I did far more vampire detecting than building. So many people came to me who had these eternal fiends in their life and many was the time I helped them to loosen their hold on these black bloodsuckers. For we hold them as much as they hold us, Miss Whittle."

"It sounds such a mouthful, Mr Pyne, and far too formal, why, it is giving me goosebumps, so please, call me Verity."

"Very well, and I shall be Frederick."

The two bent nearer and he took her hand and kissed it.

"Enchanted to meet you," he said, finding her violet eyes a distraction when they were upon him. She smiled and settled back in her chair whilst the story resumed.

"I am one and thirty, Miss...er, I mean Verity but at times I feel like an old man. It is a massive weight on your shoulders, this secret that vampires walk among us and rub flesh with us mere mortals."

"So, tell me, Frederick, how do you spot a vampire? Produce a clove of garlic? Strike them through the heart with a stake and see if they die? Get a mirror and ask them to pose for a reflection?"

"I see you know a little, Verity, but that is the old and conventional view of these creatures and, sadly, it is no longer that simple. They have become immune to water, impervious to garlic and a stake through the heart can only be performed when the final weapon has been unleashed...love."

"Love? How can that help?"

"It works on a different vibration. It creates an aura that physically strangles a vampire and they cannot breathe. The vibration is much higher than their energy, which is of a lower, base variety. They simply cannot tolerate the purity of the emotion and the unselfish nature of it drowns them in the light of virtue. In short, they shrivel up and die and then comes the stake through the heart to finally give them the peace they deserve."

"I...I still do not understand."

"Their hold upon us is fear, Verity, and this fear feeds them, as surely as the blood they drink. Love is an alien poison to them and destroys them utterly with its high vibration. Like inverse magnetic energy, they are repelled by it but its power is too great...it overcomes, time after time. The stake and the mallet are merely figureheads and the tools of my trade. My father used chisels and hammers to carve his words on stone but I use them to stop the suffering of my adversaries. For, suffer they do."

"But how does all of this relate to my uncle? My father visited him here once, I own, but my mother and I never did. He came back with a white face and did not go again. He refused to talk about it in front of me but I heard some of the talk to my mother and it was hardly sanguine. They both believed the man was mad and left it at that."

Ignoring her question, Frederick was in full flow. "Love has power that transcends death and it can restore them too, so that they can reach heaven's gate, though what St Peter makes of them, I do not know. One can only hope he looks favourably on these lost souls. Yes, love will prise a vampire's grip from life. The Undead can never be truly happy as their affliction, for such it is, leads them to a state of constant unrest. Even when they sleep they covet and they do not rest. The blood lust is overwhelming and like no addiction we will ever know, to food, tobacco or drugs. Even after they have fed and are replete with blood, their brain is craving the next meal and looking for it too."

"You sound as though you have a certain amount of pity for them, Frederick."

"I do, and if there is no-one else there to love them and send them to eternal rest, then I will do it. I will open the lotus flower on their head and send in the divine light of love. As much as I hate what they do, with the constant predation on innocent men through the centuries, I feel their pain. Well, how could I not?

"But your uncle, Verity, to come back to your question. A villager here summoned me, six months ago and more, but I was fighting the winged demon in Wales and could not attend for nigh on five weeks. Strange comings and goings here indeed and all studied and recorded by this man. Here is what he said, as I remember it in his letter.

"Weird happenings in our village," he wrote, "Two maidens now found on the moor, just outside the settlement, with puncture wounds on their neck and totally bloodless. The priest here was horrified and refused to bury them in sacred ground, having seen such things before and knowing they would walk."

"And I saw them at the crossroads, full four weeks ago, Verity, on a night with a blazing moon. I followed them to your uncle's house and saw them gain admittance. He was dead by then, of course, but lay in state for those demons to worship him as one of their own. Only the talk was then that he died from anaemia, with scarce a drop of blood in his body; so someone above him, a man he was heard to call 'Master', must have sent him to hell first. But he will walk ,Verity, in fact, men have seen him, and he meets up with these maidens and they dance. And of course, when I say your uncle was dead, he is as dead as the Undead can be. I believe he violated some sort of vampire code and his Master took him for fodder. It is likely they all fed from him but why, I do not know. On that night, when the maidens visited, I did not see him but the bats crawled thickly on the house front and I knew he could be among them."

Verity felt her face flush and her heart raced. Her secret! "I...I think I desire a break for refreshment, Frederick. It is so much to take in."
"It is indeed."
"I have no bell here, so I must retire to the kitchen to summon Liddy to prepare us some tea. You will excuse me?"
"Of course. It is thirsty work this tale-telling and a cup would be very welcome, thank you."
'And I need space and time to come to terms with this and with what I saw. Why, the man has described it exactly,' thought Verity, leaving the room. 'To think, one of those bats could have been my uncle,' she shuddered, 'And heaven only knew what he would have done had he gained admittance,' She touched her neck briefly.

Within a minute, she was in the sanctuary of the kitchen and Liddy was baking. The homely aura this created gave her at least a temporary sense of relief. She collapsed on a chair and cried,

"Tea, Liddy, for the gentleman and myself – if I can swallow a drop. He KNOWS, Liddy – he knows about the bats. He stood on a night with a blazing moon and they crawled thickly over the house front, just as I saw them last night."

"Did he, miss? I mean, do you believe him?" Liddy's eyes avoided her mistress's but Verity was not fooled.

"You know something, Liddy, don't you? You said you had heard tales of this place, so were they concerning vampires?"

"I heard tales, it is true, but I did not believe them. Tales of orgies with village maidens and your uncle. He was supposed to pay them but...I don't know, and then they vanished."

"And were found dead and bloodless on the moor, Liddy, such as Frederick has told me?"

"I...I heard they were found and suicide was talked about, so the priest would not bury them in hallowed ground, miss, but let them lie by the crossroads, as is seemly for those that take their own lives hereabouts."

"And you know no more, Liddy?"

"No, miss, I don't."

Verity gave a great sigh. What had she inherited here? A nest of vampires? Something that was way beyond her comprehension, that was for sure.

"Bring the tea in, Liddy, and some of those little cakes you have just made. I must get back to my guest."

As she returned, her heart sank within her and the future indeed seemed black and haunted by the figures of the Undead who seemed to surround her. Their long shadows reached out to her and she felt their menace.

27

CHAPTER THREE

"I am very grateful that you have seen fit to give me this audience, Verity," said Frederick, as they drank their tea.

"It seems my life, and possibly that of my maid, may depend on it," she replied, "Although I find your story incredible, I have to own that, last night I did see the bats you described, crawling on my wall, just opposite the window. Not only that but I could hear their sharp little voices and it terrified me."

"What did they say? Could you understand them?"

"Sadly, yes. They screamed for 'fresh blood' and a number of them tried their luck at the window, fluttering and banging at the pane..."

"You must NEVER let them in, no matter how much they cry. They are creatures of the night and, as such, governed by unfathomable instincts to feed and kill."

"They...they mesmerised me, I will own, and I felt compelled to draw up the sash but my maid was with me and she stopped such rash actions."

"So, she saw them too?"

"No, they had gone by the time I woke her but I still thought I could hear the flutter of bony wings in the distance."

"You must draw the curtains or blinds every night and make sure you never give them an audience. Hypnotism is indeed one of their - how shall we put it - 'tricks' and they perform it very well."

Verity shuddered. Bat fodder, she thought.

"So, I must be wary of going out at night here too?"

"Indeed. Few villagers do after dark and, if they do, they are armed with shovels and sticks to ward off the creatures."

"So, it is common knowledge hereabouts?"

"It is a silent secret few would ever talk about and thus, it is confined to the village but those passing through take a massive risk, did they but know it. Word will get out, Verity, unless we can kill these devils before they spread."

"And you think you can do that? It is possible?"

"I don't know…I am not sure how many we are talking about. Certainly the two maidens are now part of the legion of the Undead, and your uncle. Anyhow, I shall finish my story and then take up no more of your time."

"After I had followed those bitches of Satan - oh, sorry, miss, do pardon my language, sometimes my fervour gets the better of my manners - I turned my attention to your uncle. As yet, I did not know he was one of the great Undead but I found out he had been lately buried and on visiting the grave it was quiet and undisturbed. A simple, wooden cross marked his resting place and all was tranquil. No mourners had adorned it with flowers or wreaths."

"I sent orders that everything was to be made tidy and decent, Frederick. Of course, it made inroads on the money he left but, although we were never close and I saw him perhaps six times, the old boy deserved a decent send off, even though few attended."

"You have seen his final resting place?"

"No, not yet, but I gave the stone mason instructions to begin the headstone last week."

Frederick continued with his tale.

"I came up here once I knew Mr Whittle had quit the place but I could not gain admittance and a man peered out when I knocked and told me, in no uncertain terms, that he would call the police were I to remain. Then, as I was leaving, another man hailed me, coming, it seemed, from the direction of the house.

"Sir! Sir," he called, and I slowed down and waited for him. He told me that old Mr Whittle had died from blood loss, although there was no sign of any wounds. He obviously found it strange and he seemed to search my face for answers, as though I knew something. When I asked who he was, he mentioned having a doctorate in medicine, and that he had come across such deaths before in far-flung countries, such as Romania. He knew that I was aware of that which he spoke.

"'Sir,'" I said, "Let us not beat around the bush. We have both had experience with that to which you refer. The man was killed by a vampire and that means..."

"He, in turn, will become one of the Undead, yes," replied my companion.

"People around here already speak of huge bats sucking blood from their cattle and sheep and trying to attack their daughters. You believe this man has fallen prey to one of those? For, in truth, I was summoned to ascertain exactly what is occurring here, although I was unable to gain admittance to the property you have just quitted. Another man told me to go away, in no uncertain terms, and the man so lately dead, lived like a hermit."

"I found no clue there to what he died of," the man replied, "How did he get involved with such bloodsuckers, is my thought? Mr Whittle had not seen a doctor for many a year, it is true, and his reason for taking this house was to work towards spiritual enlightenment but somehow, that does not sit so well when you add in a vampire or two."

"It seems the vampires hit the area before Mr Whittle came but why his home should be the focus for them is beyond me. I had hoped to ascertain why."

"Blood!" cried the man, stopping in his tracks and turning to me, "Come with me, sir, and I will show you why the vampires found Mr Whittle so enchanting!"

"I thought I was finally going to gain admittance to the house, Verity, so I went along but no, we walked round the building and into the extensive gardens behind. My companion, who introduced himself as Dr Forbes, then took a key from his pocket and opened the largest of the sheds from whence came a nauseating smell. I covered my nose and tried to breathe through my mouth."

"What the hell is that?" I asked, from the depths of my pocket handkerchief.

"Blood," replied the good doctor. "Bushels and quarts and gallons of blood."

Despite the smell I was fascinated.

"Blood?" I said, "But what the hell did he want with such vast quantities of it?"

"Come and see," invited my companion.

"So, we left the vats of blood and ventured out into the garden itself, where rows and rows of vegetables and numerous fruit trees awaited us.

"He grew crops and was almost self sufficient, except when drought or extreme cold forced him to the mill to buy flour and bread," my friend informed me, "It just hit me, that smell and the constant deliveries from the slaughterhouses, a vampire's idea of heaven with food on tap. And I had heard that his harvests were stunning in both their quantity and quality. Apples as huge as footballs and marrows bigger than children!"

"So, blood was his fertiliser and no doubt he mixed it with other things to both improve the soil and swell the produce."

"Indeed. His other shed is like a chemist's lab where he must have tried things like bone meal and fish, as it stinks of both. He could, of course, sell his surplus stock and thus bring in money for the other things in life he required, such as candles."

"Very little was ever purchased, from what the villagers say and the fact that he never went abroad, apart from during the hours of darkness, seeking out others to fetch and carry what was required, can only make the man even more of an enigma. I hope to find the individuals who helped him and interview them, so that more comes to light."

"It seems simple, really. The man moved into the area, unaware of the vampires who frequented the darkness and, in ignorance, came to buy and use the very thing they prized above all else…blood."

"And would animal blood suffice? I mean, I had read that it was human blood they needed and fresh too, running through veins and arteries, not stale and pungent in a vat."

"Any port in a storm I believe. How much simpler to come here to feed rather than have to stalk prey in the village or on the moors. Blood is blood at the end of the day, my friend."

31

"And so saying, he locked up the shed and we parted, with at least a window open into the tragic world of your uncle."

Frederick leant back in his chair with the air of a man who has done a good day's work. He then turned his face to his host and asked what she thought of his tale.

"For I see in your eyes there is a small flame of disbelief, even though you saw the bats for yourself. Did you tell yourself you dreamt them? Especially as your maid did not observe them. I remember you said that, by the time you called her, they had vanished."

"Quite right, Frederick, but it was indeed, one glimpse into a hellish world and I dare not leave those curtains open tonight. Yet part of me needs proof, from another pair of eyes, that I have not been hallucinating. But will they come every night and are they really after the blood stored in the sheds? I mean, are you certain it is still there?"

"This was not so long ago, Verity, and even nearer in time, was the farm labourer I encountered early one morning, as I came back from the cross roads, where I had waited to see if the maidens showed up again."

"And did they?"

"No, sadly, but I met a man going to work at about 5 o'clock who was in a state of shock and disbelief. He approached me and I could hear him muttering. "Was it him?" he asked himself, "Was it him, for the man be dead and new in the earth?"

"Man,"I called out after him, for he would have shuffled by and not noticed me, so great was his distraction,

"What have you seen to make your eyes so huge and your pupils dilate as though you had drunk of opiates?"

"The man stopped and looked at me, as though he did not know of my existence, then he began to talk and out came his tale. It seemed he had strayed off the well known path to work, in the dark, and had encountered a man matching the description of your uncle, wearing a dark cloak that hid his face and shoulders."

'Who are 'ee? Who goes there this time of the morning?' the man asked the stranger. No answer. In fact the man appeared to ignore the farm labourer, although the questioner felt keen eyes upon him. The stranger walked by and, just then, a shaft of moonlight hit him and the labourer turned back to see the cloak thrown off and the features of Mr Whittle become visible."

'Why, Mr Whittle, the village is telling a tale of you being dead and not only dead but buried too. How can that be since you look as much flesh and blood as I am?'

The stranger smiled - a long, slow smile and held out his hand.

'Feel me, sir, if you doubt my humanity.'

"His hand was cold and clammy, the worker told me, just like touching a piece of raw fish. He withdrew his fingers and heard Mr Whittle laughing, as he drifted off into the darkness."

"And he was certain it was my uncle? Had he seen the man much?"

"Apparently he saw him a few times at the mill where he often worked. In fact, he may have been the last man to see your uncle alive, for Mr Whittle ventured up to the mill a few days before he was discovered dead, so who knows? But he was adamant it was your uncle. He may have been terrified, but nothing could persuade him otherwise. No 'trick of the moonlight' for him and no daydreaming either. He would have sworn on his children's lives it was Mr Whittle."

"And did you believe him?"

"I did and, the day after that, a lady of good standing had been out late, looking for her dog who had run off; she came across the same creature in almost exactly the same spot. She had a lantern and tried to raise it to the man's eyes but he damned her and, suddenly, she found he was gone. I spoke to her only yesterday and, despite never having seen your uncle, she gave a very thorough description of him; I have no reason to disbelieve her either."

Verity was silent for a few minutes. That her uncle would seek her out if this was true, she had no doubt. Was he not one of the bats, trying vainly to get in last night, and would he be there tonight? She shivered and leant to make up the fire, which had died down whilst the story was being told but the cold she felt was deep inside.

"So, what do you want to do now, Frederick? I mean, how does one proceed with a vampire?"

"If you would like me to, I can come tonight and sit in the bedroom with you - with your maid there of course, for propriety - and we can watch together to see if the creatures come. But first, I would like to check on the sheds to see if the blood vats are intact. Your uncle must have ordered them frequently and, despite the fact that there will be no more, I think we could use them as a bargaining tool."

"But surely they should be thrown away and thus the connection broken?"

"I do not think it will be that simple, Verity. I wish it was. Your uncle, if he is one of the Undead, will be grounded here and forced to return. God knows how many of the other demons are following him! The maidens are just two that I know of and every time they bite they create one more. Better that they drink the blood we have stored here, than ours!"

He rose to go and ascertain if the vats were still full but Verity pre-empted him.

"I will come too," she said simply, and called for Liddy to bring her cloak.

Two minutes later, they were in the garden. This was all new to Verity and she gazed around her, anxious to see the full extent of what she had inherited. Liddy told her she had only been to the tiny kitchen garden, where fragrant herbs were grown; thyme, parsley, lemon balm and tarragon, to name but a few.

"My uncle was a man of Nature, that I must say," she told Frederick, as they climbed the steps up to the sheds.

"Indeed, Verity, I had heard that when I first began making enquiries about him. He loved his garden and growing things, and he sold the full harvests easily among the locals. I do not know when he encountered these demons. It seems,

34

during the last year, things changed drastically and the quiet retreat he had created here was broken. I would hesitate to tell you exactly what went on at these gatherings but I am convinced, by then, he had been bitten and the vampire curse was upon him."

"I remember him, from being a child, holding forth on the rights of Nature and her creatures. He abhorred hunting of any kind and would take injured wildlife in to nurse back to health. Hard as I am trying,0 I cannot think of him as a bad man."

"And neither should you. When we meet him, I want you to think of him with love in your heart. In fact, I want you to surround him with that love and thus, finish off the part of him that remains. He has been taken over by a parasite. Your uncle has gone and in his place is this sick, twisted creature with a lust for blood but if you bring up the image of your uncle as he was, in your mind, then we may yet sleep peacefully in our beds."

"But must we…I mean, do I have to meet him?" cried Verity, somewhat shocked at the idea.

"I believe he will come back here for the blood, should the vats be intact of course."

"Can't we just pour them away, or have them carried to the moors so the vampires may feed there?"

"But then their reign will be eternal, and we will both be in our graves whilst they suck our children's blood. How many there will be then, I do not know. They slaughtered a sheep last night, by the crossroads; some poor soul found its corpse, totally bloodless, with its throat sporting the usual telltale marks. The farmers here cannot sustain such losses, day after day. One sheep would possibly feed one or two of them, maybe a few more, but we look to be facing a good half dozen."

"And is your plan to lure them back here for the blood and kill them all single-handed?"

"I have performed such acts alone before but I was hoping a high-spirited lady like yourself would at least assist me with your uncle. I hesitate to put you in any danger, Verity, but I know it is so much easier when a relation sends the love. The others, I will gladly tackle alone. Who the Master is here, I have no idea."

"And is there always a Master? Did my uncle have one then?"

"It is likely. Even amidst the Undead there is a hierarchy. Your uncle must have been groomed by someone before he had his first bite. Oh, I jest at times about this, Verity, but it is deadly serious, if you catch my meaning."

They were in the shed by now, and Frederick was checking the vats.

"They are the same as last time I was here, so the vampires have obviously not broken in but that will merely be a matter of time. The smell of the blood will call them and, if they cannot feed elsewhere, this will be their next meal. These vats would feed a few so, if we use them as decoys, we shall then know the number we are dealing with."

"You mean, let them get stronger to fight us, by feeding them. Surely that can't be right, Frederick? I would rather destroy the whole lot and find some other way to slaughter the creatures."

"But we need to see what we are up against, Verity. It may be just your uncle and the two maidens but I have my doubts. I propose we watch in your chamber tonight and then tomorrow, put one of these vats out in the garden and see what comes."

"You mean, watch from afar?"

"Yes. Do not worry, your safety is my prime concern and I will not endanger you if I can help it."

Verity felt a thrill run up and down her spine but whether it was of excitement or terror, she could not say; she felt controlled by both states in equal measure.

They locked up the shed and left. 'How fast things are moving,' thought Verity, 'I have only been here one day and already my future is challenged. I had hoped to merge into the country air here and rest, after the tragic labour of nursing my parents, but it is not to be.'

36

Frederick paused by the back door, took her gloved hand and kissed it.

"I leave you, my dear, to compose yourself and rest, in order to face whatever transpires tonight. You can be sure our enemies are sleeping, oblivious to our plans but, when they wake, they will need to feed and the bloodlust may draw them here as themselves or in the guise of bats. It seems the shed is secure for now but I cannot guarantee it will remain so, as the creatures could break in if no other food offers itself. They would rather have warm living blood, for sure, so another sheep on the moors may suffice; if they can find one that is. I shall not be alone tonight, Verity, as I shall bring my learned friend, Lawrence Grey, who has lived in this area for nigh on sixty years and has seen such things as this, rise and fall. You have no objection? He is a noble man and a wood turner by trade, before he retired that is. He has come out of this retirement to help me fight these vampires."

"Anyone who is going to help us fight these fiends is welcome here, Frederick," Verity replied. In her heart, she prayed that not a single bat would be visible tonight. 'But what if these vampires came as themselves,' a part of her wondered, surely that would be worse than any bat? 'I want it to all be a bad dream,' she thought. She was aware her next job was to tell Liddy and gain her support for the coming vigil.

Frederick was speaking again.

"So that you are not in any danger, I politely request that you and your maid remain in the house at all times, from dusk," he said, scanning the cloudy sky, "And remember, darkness is early in January and very often sudden. Do not stray too far from the well known paths, if ever you walk across the moors."

"I propose NEVER to wander about under cover of darkness until you have destroyed every bloodsucker for miles around!" Verity told him.

They parted at the kitchen door and Verity went to find Liddy. The young girl was sweeping up in the parlour and rose as her mistress entered the room.

"I can see by your face, miss, that you are not happy with all Mr Pyne has told you."

"Do you know him Liddy or know of him at all?"

"I have heard he has a good standing in the village, miss, and he pays his bills regular-like and bothers no-one."

"He has bothered me very much with his questions and narrative, Liddy. But one problem rankles, can I trust him?"

"I would say so, miss...yes. I heard he came to investigate the weird goings-on here but not a word did he say to anyone as he rambled round the area."

"He is a gentleman's son, is he not, Liddy?"

"Yes, miss, and his home is in London, so he told one elder of the village, but he is rarely there as his main job is as an investigator of the occult."

"And will you be by my side tonight, Liddy? Can I ask you to keep me company downstairs whilst Mr Pyne and his friend watch upstairs?"

"Yes, miss, providing I get some sleep this afternoon, as we had a disturbed night you may recall. But, of course, that's if you see fit to release me from service for a few hours?"

"That is not a problem as I thought we would both retire at 4 and get up at 9, since Mr Pyne talks of coming at 10. He will want feeding, of course."

"The bread is rising, miss, and I made more cakes on the griddle and some soup from the vegetables I gleaned from the garden earlier."

Verity walked up and down, clasping and unclasping her hands, as though in mental anguish.

"And tonight will prove whether he speaks the truth or it is all a joke, played on a newcomer for a bet!"

"I can't think that, miss – not at all!"

"But vampires, Liddy, and my uncle, one of them! Why, I wanted to think of him safe at Abraham's bosom!"

"He may yet be, miss, if Mr Pyne uses his stake and mallet!"

"Ah. Were you listening at the door or do you know more of vampires than you have admitted to?"

"I have heard plenty in the village since Mr Pyne came, miss, but I haven't heard one bad word against him and only disbelief as to why he came."

"So, people do not believe him?"

"They don't want to, miss, no they don't, but they can't close their eyes to what is happening here."

"And neither can we, Liddy, since it concerns every brick in this house and, as such, directs my future. So, knowing what you know, will you watch with me tonight?"

"I will, miss, and I am not afraid if Mr Pyne is there. He killed four man-eating vampires in the wilds of Wales less than six weeks ago and sent another three to meet their maker in Norfolk, on Halloween."

"But what will the village say about this if it is true and I, the man's niece? Will they drive me out, do you think and more to the point, should I, in all honesty, go?"

"I think you should stay, miss, and see what transpires. I believe we are in safe hands with Mr Pyne."

"I pray you are right. But we must feed our bodies, if our souls are to be strong enough to withstand whatever comes our way tonight."

"Watching is Mr Pyne's way at first, miss. He will only strike when he is good and ready."

"You seem to know a lot about him, Liddy?"

The maid blushed a little.

"Well, there has been much talk over such a handsome and eligible man in the vicinity. A few of the more – what shall I say – 'improper' females have been offering their swan-like necks for him to bite!"

"Liddy! That is scandalous!"

"Sorry, miss, I should have said that he has caused a bit of a flutter among the female hearts of the district, probably because women outnumber men in this region."

"Do not repeat such gossip again, Liddy. Mr Pyne is a virtuous man, with family no doubt!"

"No wife, miss, to speak of, married to his job it seems."

"What, tracking down and slaughtering vampires?"

"I think he prefers to view it as saving them, miss, from an eternity of misery and thus dispatching them to the gates of heaven. What St Peter makes of them, and whether they get in, is another matter, miss, and between them and God."

"So, you believe all this heaven and hell business then?"

"I do, miss, as far as we make our own heaven or hell here, on this earth plane, by the deeds we perform."

"So, where do vampires stand in this? Do they deserve eternal damnation for the sins they have performed whilst in the grip of this so-called 'blood fever'?"

"I hope they are pardoned, miss – truly I do!"

Verity was silent for a moment, but her thoughts were dark and tragic.

"So, my uncle is either to be raised to the ranks of glory or cast down into the unremitting fires of hell?"

"I doubt it is as clear a division as that, miss. I have read widely..."

"You can read, Liddy? Many of your standing cannot."

"Oh yes, miss, my mother taught me when I was six. She was a lady's maid but it did not stop her getting on in the world. She is now head cook at Porter Hall and, although my father sank to rest after a thatching accident, she has gone on to marry a younger man and seems very happy."

"I am very pleased for her, Liddy. I hope, one day, you and I may be happy here."

"I trust we will in time, miss, once the vampires are gone."

They retired to rest, but Verity could not sleep. She was not used to sleeping in the day and besides, she did not feel tired but wide awake and fretful. What would the coming night bring?

"I have been here but one day and look what has unfolded," she told herself. Calming her racing mind, she counted the sheep on the moors as they appeared to her and gradually, slowly her hold on consciousness broke. She slept.

CHAPTER FOUR

Dimly, through the parting mists of sleep, Verity became conscious of a hand shaking her gently and a voice reaching her from the shadowy perception of her dreams. She came to and found Liddy by her side with a candle.

"It is just gone nine, Miss. Will you partake of some...well, supper really, I suppose?"

Verity sat up and stretched her stiff limbs.

"I am not hungry, Liddy, but by all means, eat if you desire to."

"I have no appetite either, Miss."

Verity got up off the bed and reached for her shoes. Darkness engulfed the room and it felt cold.

"Liddy, bring me some more candles, for I know Mr Pyne will need some later. Is the fire lit in the parlour?"

"Yes, Miss. I have just banked it up with tea leaves, for it was glowing when I got up half an hour ago."

"And you have heard nothing? Seen nothing?"

"No, Miss, I have been busy preparing refreshments. Only the assault of the wind on the house front has disturbed me. Did you sleep?"

"Yes, thank you – after a fashion. And, mercifully, I did not dream either."

"They say you are exhausted when you do not dream, Miss, and you must be after all that travelling and barely a minute to catch your breath."

Verity noticed the curtains were drawn in the room and she was thankful for that, she did not want to look out there ever again. How can I stay here unless it is proved tonight to be some sort of prank, she thought, as she pushed cold feet into her shoes and asked Liddy for some hot water for a wash. She felt stale and grimy from sleep.

Half an hour later, she was accepting a cup of tea from Liddy when a knock came at the door. The two women looked at each other and Liddy was dispatched to answer it. A tall, thin gentleman of advancing years stood there and raised his hat to the maid.

41

"Good evening," he said, in a soft and gentle voice, "I believe I am expected? I hope Mr Pyne told you I was coming to keep him company in his vigil tonight."

"Why, Mr Grey, how nice to see you!" cried Liddy, beckoning him in. "Do you remember me? You last saw me when I was a child but Mother speaks highly of you, always. She remembers your kindness when Father had his accident."

"Well, Miss Wentworth, is it really you?" replied the gentleman, removing his hat as he entered, "You have grown into a fine young woman!"

"Thank you, sir. And I hope you are well too?"

"Perfectly, Miss Wentworth, and anxious to rid the locality of these creatures I have been watching with Mr Pyne."

"Come in and meet my mistress, sir," Liddy told him, shutting the door as the damp evening air was advancing along the hallway.

She led the gentleman into the parlour which was warm and fragrant with the flames of a fire. Verity was sitting, warming her hands when he entered but she rose and came over to him.

"Ah, so you must be the Mr Grey Frederick spoke of. I am very happy to make your acquaintance," she said, holding out her hand.

Lawrence took it gently and mentioned the pleasure was all his.

"Sit by the fire, Mr Grey."

"Lawrence," he prompted.

"Lawrence," Verity repeated, "Have you come far?"

"Just from the village, Miss Whittle, but our mutual friend, Frederick, filled me in on your background and how you came to be here."

"Yes, I have inherited this mouldy pile."

"And seemingly a lot of trouble with it too. You may wish your uncle had had another niece to leave this 'mouldy pile' to, as you so eloquently put it."

Another, sharper, knock at the door interrupted them and Liddy went off to answer it. It wanted some twelve minutes till the hour of ten but it was Frederick, in dark attire and eager to begin the vigil.

"Well, well, Lawrence – you old dog, trust you to be early to enjoy the company of two delightful ladies!"

Lawrence laughed and remarked he was rather long in the tooth for any dalliance and besides, they had an urgent mission here that took all thoughts of love out of the equation.

"Ah, but it may not always be so," replied Frederick, handing his hat and coat to Liddy with a smile, "Don't forget, if we manage to corner one of these creatures tonight, it is love we must send them, the love of the universe; it is the only thing that will destroy them."

"You have your weapons then, Frederick?"

"Yes, indeed. I never travel anywhere without them after dark," and he produced a few items from his bag to show the ladies.

"Here are the tools of a vampire hunter's trade," he held up the familiar stake and wooden mallet, almost crude in its simplicity, and then he handed over a Bible for Verity to peruse and a phial of Holy Water for Liddy to see.

"And I have wild-grown garlic to throw in front of them and confuse their way," he continued, pulling out a necklace of it.

"I have a mirror and more Holy Water," replied Lawrence, "Plus a volume of the Psalms that I like to read to them as they are departing to God."

"Heavens!" cried Verity, returning the Bible, "Do you mean to make a killing here tonight? I thought it was for observation only! Heaven forbid they should get in here!"

"Ah, you can never be sure with a vampire," replied Frederick, taking the Bible from her trembling hands, "We have planned nothing but they may have, so we cannot be sure."

"We always come prepared, Miss Whittle," endorsed Lawrence, "You just do not know."

"And now that we have terrified you ladies, would you be so good as to show us the chamber where we shall pass the night?" continued Frederick, as the clock struck ten.

Liddy took a candle from the table and asked him to follow her. Verity decided to come too and Lawrence made up the rear. They climbed the stairs, traversed the corridor and arrived at the chamber where Verity had seen the bats. "May I?" asked Frederick, gesticulating to the curtains and Verity nodded. He flicked them back but the house front that confronted them was empty, apart from a stray piece of branch that the wind had blown hither and thither and finally trapped on the small, jutting out roof below them.

"They were there," murmured Verity, as though she had to apologise for their absence. "I know I saw them. Even though by the time I called Liddy, who sleeps in the room opposite, they had gone. I did not dream it."

"And what time was it? Late I assume?" asked Frederick, his eyes darting over the scene from the window as he familiarised himself with the layout.

"Yes, midnight had struck and gone, I believe, or it could have been one o'clock but it wasn't long after we retired to sleep."

"And had you slept?" asked Lawrence, joining Frederick at the window.

"I...I think so," replied Verity, "A little." She felt suddenly confused about the whole episode. Would the men sit till daybreak and see nothing?

Lawrence pulled up a chair, and Frederick positioned himself on the windowsill itself, which was wide enough to support him.

"Now ladies, go downstairs and make up the parlour fire, then rest. We will call you if anything presents itself."

"Will you take some refreshments, sirs?" asked Liddy. She lit them a candle and put this on the bureau, where it cast long shadows in monstrous form over the bed.

"Nothing containing alcohol, please," Lawrence replied, "But some tea or coffee would be very stimulating. We need to keep clear heads and open minds."

Verity wished them good watching and then quit the room, instructing Liddy to bring up a tray of cakes and tea, and to serve some in the parlour also. To this room she repaired and sat in a chair, bolt upright, listening for the scrape of wings on stone or for one of the observers calling her name. The old house milked the silence, and only the rustle of burning embers in the fire disturbed Verity's thoughts.

Liddy brought in a tray for her mistress but Verity could scarcely swallow a drop. The cakes remained uneaten on the plate and presently, Liddy joined her.

"It wants twenty minutes to midnight, Miss, and if you wish to sleep, I will keep wakeful and call you should the men see anything."

Verity looked pensive.

"Do you think I imagined the whole thing, Liddy? My brain may have tricked me that I was awake when, in reality, I was asleep and dreaming."

"A regular nightmare, Miss, and no dream for a lady of business!"

"And why bats, I wonder? I had seen none on my journey or, indeed, any when I arrived here. Why were they deep in my subconscious?"

"Had you read about them?"

"No, Liddy, for I rarely read, although I would like to, now that my time is my own; poetry from the last century maybe..."

She did not get to finish her sentence as a knock at the door stunned her into silence. Liddy jumped up to answer it, and saw Frederick's excited face in the doorway.

"The gates of Hell are wide open and the Undead have joined us. Bats, dear ladies, bats."

Sitting in the bedroom, some minutes later, her eyes fixed on the multitude of bats crawling over the house front and occasionally trying their luck at the window, Verity knew now her dream was indeed a waking nightmare.

"There are even more of them than I saw," she said, in a voice of high alarm.

45

"The blood draws them in," replied Lawrence.

"Then I want it gone," Verity told him.

Frederick approached the window and tried to allay her fears.

"They will not get in," he affirmed, "As long as no-one opens a window or goes out there. Daylight will banish them but whilst the hours of darkness rule, they are the champions. Come dawn, they will retreat to their lairs and sleep."

"But they will be back tomorrow," cried Verity, moving away, "And the day after and the one after that and worst of all, is the terrible thought that my uncle, my own flesh and blood, is one of them!"

"We don't know that for sure," Lawrence said, "But yes, it is likely."

"And which one is he?" Verity almost shouted. She felt worked up to fever pitch and the last hope she had clung to had disintegrated before her eyes.

"Calm down, my dear lady," advised Frederick, "What you saw the other night was no figment of your imagination but, now we know, neither Lawrence nor I will rest until we rid this area of these creatures. Whatever form they come in, they will be met with the same fortitude and resistance, do not fear!"

Verity took a few deep breaths and tried to quieten her racing mind. She turned to the window again and looked intently at the crawling bats. She shivered. Their eyes! Red, glowing eyes, redolent of demons and those inhabiting the darker regions of hell! The stuff of nightmares, come to flesh!

Frederick bade her study the group closer.

"Are there any there that you feel could be your uncle?" he murmured.

"Would I know?" pondered Verity, thinking they all looked equally disgusting. Some were salivating and their spittle ran from sharp, white teeth...she grimaced.

"I think you will feel something if your eyes rest on the twisted soul of your uncle," Frederick assured her, "You may not have seen him for years but somewhere in your brain is printed the characteristics of not only his face but his soul. I have seen it before and sisters, parted at birth, have recognised their sibling purely from a turn of the head or a light in the eyes, even when their relation was in another body. Look, Verity! Look hard! We need to know if your uncle is among this colony of bats!"

Verity knew, no matter how distasteful she found this, she must keep searching, even though her eyes ached. She cast another long, lingering glance over the company. How they revolted her! Some crawled over others and fought valiantly for space. She could see by their eyes they were hungry and almost ready to turn on their fellows for the blood they craved. She swept her eyes up to the top of the building and down again and, as she did, a larger bat than the others flew down, attempting to grip the cold pane of glass between them. She saw the red, misty eyes; the rabid, fetid breath steaming up the glass and in an instant, she knew who it was. "My uncle!" she cried, as the bat fell from the window and was seen no more, "I could see into his soul as you said and it was he, or rather, what was left of him, after the creatures of the night had taken what they needed."

Frederick glanced down to where the bat had fallen. "There he goes!" he cried, as the huge wings covered the window once more and the creature rose and disappeared into the night sky.

"And you are sure?" asked Lawrence, "You recognised traits that your uncle had in life, in that bat?"

Verity turned away from the window, somewhat confused. "I...I don't know, I am not sure what I saw but it wasn't a bat. It was as if my uncle stood there, as I saw him in life; well, the last time was years ago but, yes, I am sure it was my uncle, no matter what body he inhabited."

"Some water I think please, Liddy, and take your mistress down to the parlour fire as she looks very pale. There is no need for you to remain any longer, Verity. You have done very well and now Lawrence and I will complete the vigil on our own."

"But what if he comes back? My uncle I mean?"

"We shall know him now. He may of course change bodies and appear in other forms. Beware of anyone asking for admittance after dusk has come, Miss Whittle," Lawrence told her, "Do not let anyone in, no matter how they beg, once night has come."

"You mean, he could appear in human form?"

"Yes, and he may try to solicit your pity as a child or a stray dog or cat. You must harden your heart and never, ever answer the door at night, even if he bangs on the window."

"Mark that, Liddy!" cried Verity, "The door is locked at dusk and is not to be opened unless it is one of these gentlemen." She was glad to quit the chamber and return to the parlour. Those eyes! And what possessed the man's soul now? True, he had always been eccentric, her mother told her but he had been kind and steady. Would he ever find peace?

Liddy brought her some water and made the fire up. Verity drank and recovered a little colour.

"Whatever the man has done, he does not deserve eternal damnation," she mused, more to herself than to Liddy, "I remember him as a kind man. Why, he brought me gifts both times he came to see me and apparently, when I was born, he sent a silver thimble that I still possess in my work basket. What did he do to be bitten by one of these demons? Was it the blood he was using on his crops that attracted them and did he just get in the way?"

Liddy rose from the hearth where she was sweeping up.

"I would not worry, Miss, nor spend precious time in useless pondering as Mr Pyne will sort it all out; have faith in him!"

Verity nodded.

"I hear you, Liddy, but I wonder what he can actually do against the forces of darkness? One false move and he will himself be bitten and become one of the enemy."

"But he has done this thing for quite a few years, Miss, and has yet to make, what you term, a false move. True, he watches and deliberates long and hard before he strikes but when he does, the stake goes through the heart."

"And do you think that is what he will do to my uncle? I remember him with fondness, Liddy. Yes, he was what my mother termed odd but he is still my flesh and blood after all and the nearest thing I have to a living relation in the world!"

"But he is dead, Miss, and you must remember that. They buried him on a wild, wet day only a few months ago and put a stone on top of him."

"But did he rest, Liddy? Did he ascend to heaven with the saints? No, he walks and even worse, he FLIES!"

"And the best thing for him, Miss, would be Mr Pyne's stake and the love vibration. If he saw you, why, he would have NO hesitation in biting you and drinking your blood!"

"Liddy, you paint a painful picture and one that revolts me. Do you really believe all Mr Pyne says?"

"I do, Miss, he has no reason to lie and I have heard what he told the village of past successes in Wales and Norfolk, fighting these bloodsucking demons. No-one dare walk abroad during the hours of darkness here, Miss, and shepherds have to leave their precious sheep to be preyed upon and find them bloodless and twisted the next morning."

"But is there no other way to persuade these creatures to leave?" she asked.

"With all due respect, Miss, they have no human attributes to appeal to. They have a heart, yes, but it only beats to furnish blood to different regions; it does not feel, or ache as ours does. You must view your uncle as dead and gone, and Mr Pyne's stake is the final part of his journey to heaven!"

"I hope you are right, Liddy. Hark, the men are calling again! They may require refreshment. I will try to sleep now, on the settle, but do wake me if anything occurs that requires my presence, won't you?"

Liddy departed, promising that she would, and Verity settled down against the velvet cushions. How strange they smelt, she noticed! But she was tired and all too soon, she drifted into slumber.

Only minutes into her restless sleep, she began to dream.

She was in her chamber, resting on her bed, and it was dark and cold. For some reason, the window was open and the curtains blew freely in a chilly wind that brought freezing drops of rain. She was almost asleep but the noise of the inclement weather disturbed her and she knew she must get up and shut the window as Frederick would not like it. Hadn't he warned her not to leave the window open? Why, Liddy must have done it when she was cleaning!

She made a move to get upright and became aware that she was not alone. Where the figure came from, she could not say but it was there, nevertheless, and she shrank back against the pillows.

"Why are you afraid of me?" came a voice that she did not recognise, "Are you and I not joined by blood? Yes, blood relations are we not?"

Verity looked and looked again. She could see the hooked nose and the sharp features that reminded her, all too painfully, of her father.

"Papa?" she said doubtfully.

"No, my dark angel, it is not he but you are only one step removed from the answer. It is your uncle, come to see you. Why, you rest in my house, and this was my bedroom."

"Was?" commented Verity, "Yes, they told me of your death but have you been rejected from heaven?"

"Perhaps heaven was never meant to be my home," he replied and bent towards her. She could smell the fetid odour of his breath and his red eyes filled her with alarm.

"But how you have changed," she said shakily and moved over in the bed as he sat down beside her,

"Frederick Pyne says you have been bitten by a vampire!"

The figure threw back his head and laughed and Verity saw the long, sharp, canine teeth and the blood flecked white of the eyes.

"Frederick Pyne can go to the Devil and entertain him!" he laughed, "He is a meddler in things he does not understand and he brainwashes you, I fear, with lies about my good person."

Verity felt him stroking her hair and she was terrified.

"Ah," he crooned, in a gentle voice, "I remember so well when you were a little girl, and you ran to me when I visited and asked what I had for you. Yes, you loved presents when you were small. Well, I have the most precious gift I can bestow on you. Immortality...living forever! Come and join me, Verity, share my blood and all this I can bestow on you. Yes, I left you my goods and chattels in life but how much better is this? Living forever and with just one bite! "

Verity had reached the other side of the bed and she was in a corner. There was nowhere to go and she saw him getting closer and closer.

"Ah!" he murmured, "Do you hear them sing? The creatures of the night! How they howl for you to join us! And you shall with just one..."

Verity began to scream. At first, she thought it was someone else crying out, so removed did she feel from reality, but gradually, she found she was awake and rapid footsteps approached the door and it was flung open.

Frederick stood in the doorway; his eyes searched the room but he found nothing.

"Miss Whittle!"

Verity's gasps for breath slowed down and she perceived she was in the parlour and no-one else inhabited the shadowy regions of the room.

"Frederick! I am so sorry, it was a dream. A dream? No, I mean a nightmare!"

"Who was with you, Verity? What made you scream out so in your sleep?"

Verity looked at him and shook her head in disbelief.

"It was my uncle," she whispered, "And he was trying to bite me." She felt her neck at this point and was relieved to find it was not punctured.

"What did he say?" asked Frederick, sitting down next to her on the settle and taking her hand to give her comfort.

"I...I can't remember. Yes, yes, it is coming back to me. He talked of the gifts he brought me as a child and said he had an even more special present for me...immortality."

"What happened next?" asked Frederick, anxiously.

"I was terrified by him and I tried to get away but I was in my chamber and the bed, of course, is against the wall, so I could not but I screamed so hard that I woke myself up and then you came in and..."

Frederick smoothed her ruffled, dark hair away from her face.

"He called me his 'dark angel'," she mused, "Was he really here? No, he could not have been. It was just my frantic mind that raised him."

Frederick left her side and warmed his hands by the fire.

"It is nearly dawn," he said, "And the reign of the Undead is over. Our watch is finished. When I left your chamber, only a few bats remained and those will have gone now, with the advent of light. See, the darkness has almost disappeared," he continued, folding back curtains and shutters and exposing the windows.

"You are hiding something," replied Verity, getting up from the settle, "This was no ordinary nightmare, was it, Frederick?"

He shrugged his shoulders but the arrival of Lawrence put paid to his silence.

"Tell her, sir. Tell her. She has to learn to love him or he will haunt her forever!"

Verity looked round.

"What do you mean?" she asked, "Frederick, what is he talking about?"

"His blood flows in your veins, Verity," the man replied, with a dour glance at his friend, "And he wants it, yes, he desires it more than anything else in this world or any other. What was your prevailing emotion in the dream?"

"Why, fear and loathing of course!" Verity told him, "How could it be anything else when his fetid breath coiled round my cheek and his cold, red eyes fell upon me, as though I was his prey."

"Which you were, of course."

"Exactly! How can a hunted deer feel anything else but fear when the dogs are almost upon it? Why, the poor animal is as likely to die from fright as from exhaustion!"

Frederick shook his head.

"No," he said, coming back to her side, "No. What did I tell you earlier? Do you remember? Yes, the stake and the garlic and the Holy Water but what else did I say would protect you?"

Verity was confused.

"I don't know..." she began, then suddenly realisation dawned, "You talked of the love vibration! You said you could kill a vampire just by loving him!"

"Exactly!" cried Lawrence, "Your dream was no accident. When you were upstairs and saw the bat you pronounced was your uncle, what were your emotions then?"

"Why, I was horrified and repulsed," she replied, seeing what the man was getting at, "I tried to see the good in him and think of him with the fondness of youth but Liddy told me not to view him that way, as he was one of the Undead. That, of course, filled me with fear." She turned to them both.

"My nightmare was no coincidence, no picture of an overwrought mind or imagination. My uncle felt my fear and he fed on it, didn't he? It gave him the power to appear to me in my sleep and almost the power to bite me, to make me one of the Undead. And you are going to say that he can do it at any time if I exhibit fear for him, if I think about him with fear, if I send my fear out to him, aren't you?"

Lawrence nodded.

"You understand us," he said at last, when silence had reigned for a few moments.

"So, you want me to think of him with love, don't you? I must send him love in order to protect myself. Do you know that this definitely works?"

Frederick nodded his head.

"We know it works," he told her, "We don't really know why it works, apart from the fact that love is the only thing stronger than death. We see love as a pink light, almost a mist, that you can surround a vampire with and with that vibration, the essence of evil is destroyed. Can you do it, Verity? Can you keep the monster away, until we have destroyed him? Is your mind stronger than your fear?"

Verity nodded.

"I can," she said, with conviction, "And I must."

CHAPTER FIVE

"You must take this seriously, Liddy, and put aside all thoughts of gossip or scandal, do you hear me?"

"Yes, Miss. It is just I wanted to tell you what Mr Haddon said about Mrs Feeby, even though he has met her for the last five nights by the pig killer's house..."

"Liddy!"

"Sorry, Miss. Yes, I shall clear my mind and join you. If it puts your uncle one step nearer heaven, it is worth it!"

"What? Worth missing out on gossip?"

"Yes, Miss, as I can tell you after the ritual."

"Liddy! You are incorrigible!"

"Sorry, Miss, I don't know what that is!"

"Never mind, just join your thoughts with mine. It is more about the power I give him, when I send out fear and negative emotions, that I am concerned about. That dreadful nightmare cannot be repeated. It was as though he stood, flesh and blood, in my chamber!"

"So do you find it hard to sleep in there now, Miss?"

"Yes, Liddy, I do."

"Then you may swap with me if you like?"

"But your room is half that size, Liddy!"

"That is so, Miss, but it looks out over the garden and not the house front!"

"I shall persevere and make sure I put the blue cloak of protection around me as Frederick has suggested."

"He is very attentive to you, Miss, isn't he and the village is bound to notice? You could be the next piece of gossip, I fear!"

"Liddy! I insist you leave the village in ignorance of our comings and goings. It does not concern them. He is a man on a mission and, in truth, I am his employers!"

"I don't think he sees it that way, Miss, he is a free spirit."

"Exactly, and once this group of vampires have been sent to heaven, with a curse on their lips, he will be gone after another!"

"Yes, and with a wistful look in his eyes and a heart on the verge of breaking!"

"Liddy! I know that you are young and fanciful but I cannot have you repeating falsehoods like that anywhere, including here. And you are to keep your tongue quiet when you go into the village."

"Very well, Miss, but I still think it is a shame not to see what is welling up in Mr Pyne's blue eyes!"

"Not another word, Liddy and I mean it. We must get on."

It was a week later and Verity and Liddy were performing their love ritual, which always seemed to be delayed by scandal or gossip. The young maid loved a tale and, as her mistress found out, she was very prone to embroidery.

"Now, Liddy, hold hands with me, close your eyes and help me bring in the eternal love of the universe." They did so, although Liddy frequently opened one eye to see if her mistress really was concentrating.

"We come together in our precious home with the everlasting power of love and we send that love out to the world to triumph over evil. In particular we send it out to my uncle, Richard Whittle, knowing that he has not passed into the light but is trapped between worlds. We ask that this love loosens the hold evil has upon him and we send it with pure hearts. Will it now, Liddy and send him a cloud of pink light, so it may surround him in its clinging mist. And now we see it infiltrating his body, sinking into his soul, which draws it in like Holy Water. Ah, yes, love is the soul's food and his soul craves it! It colours his very being and runs through his veins. We send this every minute of every day, Amen."

"Say Amen, Liddy," her mistress continued.

"Sorry, Miss. Amen...I was thinking what we were going to have for tea."

"Well you shouldn't be. How can this work if you do not put your heart into it?"

Verity took her hands away and the two broke up.

"I think I would like some more of those little griddle cakes, since you insist on putting that thought in my head!

Flavoured with that jam you found in the larder which was so good, even Frederick remarked on it."

"Did he, indeed?" replied Liddy, sitting back in her chair. "I noticed he ate six."

"And do you usually count the number of cakes my guests eat?"

"Well, Mr Lawrence ate four."

Verity raised her eyebrows. The fact that Liddy was eight years younger than her was glaringly obvious at times.

"I would say Mr Frederick is becoming more than a guest, Miss."

"Would you? I hope this is not the sort of thing you repeat in the village?"

"Oh no, Miss, it was merely an observation."

"Then keep it to yourself please, and away to begin your chores!"

"Yes, Miss."

It had been an interesting week Verity mused, and Frederick had decided, after observing the comings and goings of the bats for seven nights, that it was time to move on. Tonight, he proposed to lay a trail of blood to the shed and see exactly who turned up. Lawrence and he would be installed in the shed with all the tools of their trade to protect them, whereas the women would be watching from Liddy's bedroom.

There had been other reports of sheep with deep puncture wounds in their necks, and their bodies drained of every drop of blood, so Frederick nodded and said,

"So, they have fed but, as sure as day follows night, they will yearn for the life force again and we have it in abundance!"

Dull days in the first part of the month of January brought darkness early to cottage doors and when four o'clock rang out, the land could barely be distinguished from the navy blue sky. Verity felt very restless. All afternoon she could not sit still but walked up and down the house, picking things up and putting them down, her mind racing.

"I don't know what is the matter with me, Liddy, indeed I don't!" she confided to the maid after lunch had been cleared away, and she had eaten very little. Frederick and Lawrence came at three to bait the snare, and Verity and Liddy had watched them from Liddy's bedroom window.

"I find it all very repulsive," murmured Verity, as she saw the blood running from the vats and along the path that led eventually to the moor, "And the smell is hardly conducive to a healthy appetite either."

"It will stir a vampire's appetite alright," replied Liddy, with a smile. Blood and guts did not bother her at all, having been brought up to dismember chickens at an early age. Verity, however, was squeamish and rarely ate meat, if she could avoid it.

Just before dusk asserted itself, Verity went out to see how the men were getting on. It was a raw, grey day but the sky was clearing now and Verity thought there would be a frost later on. She found January very depressing, with the bright lights of Christmas behind them and still months of darkness before spring came to delight the world with new life. The trees dripped water, and there was no trace of wind to stir their claw-like branches.

Frederick looked up at the crunch of her footsteps on the gravel around the shed. He came out to greet her.

"Will you really be safe in here if one of those creatures comes tonight?" she asked, shivering at the cold and damp of the building.

"Yes, have no fears for us. As long as we keep our wits about us and our tools of the trade to hand, we will be fine," Frederick told her.

"And you still think my uncle may come to you, seeing as this was his place of residence whilst alive?"

"For a free meal – yes, I do. And then we will get some measure of him and his power."

"You think he is controlled by another then?"

"Possibly he is at the beck and call of the Master or who he calls the Master, anyway. The vampire foreman, to you and I."

"And women?" asked Verity, "Can they be vampire foremen too?"

58

"By all means," replied Frederick, "We dealt with a huge Welsh temptress back in the valleys, didn't we, Lawrence."

"And don't forget the two women you followed from the crossroads to here a few weeks back," said Lawrence. "They will be somewhere in the hierarchy."

"They are on my list to be destroyed," nodded Frederick.

Verity shivered again. He talked of it so lightly, killing and taking life, but she knew he had to, for the sake of the innocent humans these blood suckers preyed on.

"Will you have a light tonight, to see if they are coming?" she asked.

"Yes, Miss, we have a slatted lantern that we can open as necessary. Vampires recoil from light, so it can be used to frighten them, should they get into the shed with us," Lawrence told her.

"And food? And drink? You will take that in the parlour, or shall I send Liddy out with tea and cakes?"

"We will come to you," Frederick told her, "Nothing may happen and a meal or a cup of tea will help pass the hours. The carefully laid trail may go cold."

"Yes, indeed," Lawrence agreed, "They may be after other prey."

"But at some time, they will find this blood. True, it may not be as fresh as they would like but a stale loaf of bread is still succour to a starving man!"

Verity wished them luck and went in, telling Liddy she was going to rest for a few hours in her room but, try as she might, sleep would not come. She tossed and turned and, though her body was tired, her mind refused to slow down. What if Frederick got bitten? She acknowledged that he was dear to her heart, although she rejected Liddy's gentle teasing on the subject. The village must not know his mission here and if they wanted to talk...well, let them. Verity had never been swayed by right or duty. She did as her heart and mind told her and very often her heart ruled her head, sometimes with disastrous results.

Liddy came in at ten, just as the men were shutting themselves into the shed.

"Shall we watch from my room, Miss? I mean, I don't suppose anything will happen on this first night. Mr Frederick seems to think it will take a few vigils to stir the creatures."

"But surely the blood will draw them in? Didn't Frederick tell me that he cut himself once when these demons were about and they lusted after him immediately?"

"That was true, Miss, and the creatures can smell blood over a mile away, Mr Lawrence said. But fresh blood is what they prefer and what we are offering is tired and stale."

"Hence killing the sheep on the moors, then. It seems every day, more poor animals are found, drained to the bone."

"Well, I hope Mr Frederick's plan works, Miss, and seeing as neither of us can sleep, let us go and watch."

However, six o'clock rang out, and nothing had been drawn to the blood, not a single bat haunted the house front. It was most disappointing and the constant vigil sapped strength and energy. Coming in from the shed, Frederick proclaimed his nerves were taut with anticipation. Furthermore, the blood had soaked into the ground and an early morning shower had washed it away too. Going out at midday, when it was drier, Verity could see no trace of it, and any smell that lingered was combined with the wet fragrance of rotting leaves and plants. She cast her eyes over the produce in the garden; it was certainly well stocked with winter vegetables. Suddenly, the dry rustling of raspberry canes made her gasp. What had disturbed them? There was no breeze and, for a moment, Verity considered taking to her heels and running but then a high-pitched 'meow' made her look again. A small, black cat crouched among the dry canes and evidently, expected a cuff or kick for his presence there, judging by the way he flinched.

Verity was enchanted as she always was by animals. She bent down and called to the desperate creature,

"Puss, puss…come here then," It could be noted that she used a different, more gentle tone to animals, than she did to people. When faced with the two, Verity Whittle preferred her friends to have fur.

The cat ran to her for a stroke, and she was appalled to feel his backbone and ribs, confirming he was much too thin. Picking him up in tender arms she carried him indoors, her vigil forgotten in the desire to help her new friend.

"Liddy! Liddy!" she called, depositing the cat with great care by the fire. "Liddy, we have a hungry guest, so you must come and cut up some raw meat for him, and fill a bowl with fresh water too."

Liddy hurried in and cast her eyes over the small feline. "Lord's sake, Miss, 'tis a witch's familiar! It looks just like the one Farmer Willow stoned away last week, as it was spying on him and curdled the milk and blighted the crop in the bud. We shall have nothing but bad luck in the house if you let that in!"

"Stuff and nonsense!" cried her mistress, with ire, "How can you believe such rubbish? He is a cat and he is lost and hungry, that is all."

"But, Miss, his coat is black!"

"And what of that? How can a colour jinx anyone?"

Liddy tried to quote tales she had heard of black cats turning into witches but Verity held up her hand and would have none of it.

"Do my bidding please, Liddy, and at once. Our guest is hungry."

Reluctantly, the maid went to fetch food but could be heard muttering,

"A white one, yes, even a tabby, but one as black as coal? Well, mistress will regret giving that house room when she is struck down by the ague! Wait till Mr Frederick sees it!"

But Frederick made no comment on the creature, save giving him a scratch behind the ears as he lay on the mat by the fire, replete from his meal. It was Verity who brought the subject up.

"I have a new companion, Frederick, as you can see, although Liddy wrings her hands with foreboding and affirms we are all jinxed, with doom and gloom descending on the household!"

61

"I have heard such nonsense before," replied her human guest, offering the cat a small piece of cake, which he declined in a genteel fashion. "I have seen innocent creatures, such as this one, stoned because of the hue of their fur, by people who should know better. As if colour can affect a cat! Any elderly woman who craves the delightful company of one of these black felines causes tongues to wag, and she is then condemned as a witch!"

"Ah...I hope they will not name me so!"

"Rest assured, my dear Verity, you are much too young and beautiful to be labelled so!"

"Well, whatever is said, the little creature is going to stay and I have called him Jet, after the precious stone he resembles and which I have here in my pendant. It suits him, don't you think?"

Frederick agreed and turned his mind to other more pressing matters. The blood was not attracting the creatures he wanted and sadly, night two was to prove as barren as night one. After night three produced no sniff of a vampire, even Lawrence was worried, and he began to think of other plans. Besides which, they only had four more vats of blood.

The sheep on the moor, however, were being decimated and most farmers, bewailing their losses, brought their flocks in so the blood suckers would have to go further and further to find fresh blood. And all the time there was a trail of the substance on tap in the back garden. Frederick thought eventually, at least one of them would come.

"Their blood lust can never be satisfied," Lawrence said, a few hours later, as they prepared a fresh trail yet again and were fortunate to find dry weather. They sprinkled the floor of the shed liberally, and put a bucket of blood outside the wooden building.

"We are all ready," Frederick replied, placing his trusty stake and mallet by his side, "Holy water is blessed and now, we put our hands together and ask for God's protection this coming night."

"Nothing regarding a vampire should be undertaken lightly and without the Lord's cloak of light covering you. Join us,"

Lawrence asked Verity, as she was with them, "Then go safely back to the house and make sure all the windows and doors are bolted and locked."

Verity took Lawrence's hand and Frederick gave her his and the three bowed their heads in prayer. Verity was surprised to find what a deeply religious man Frederick was and her opinion of him rose. She squeezed his hand with genuine affection and concentrated on the task before her. "Lord, we are but your servants, and as we go forth this night, guide and guard our footsteps, so we may walk in your Holy Light and overcome the evil we face. Surround us with your love and may it never, ever fail us but go before us like a bright, guiding star. Oh, Lord, there is a dreadful darkness in this village, and we seek to destroy it and bring your peace back to the people here. Help us to achieve this. Amen." "Amen," murmured Verity and Lawrence and they all dropped hands and broke apart.

Verity left the shed with some misgivings. She knew both of the men expected to be busy tonight but one false move and they would be vampire fodder themselves.

"Guard and guide them Lord," she whispered, as the words of the prayer washed over her.

Inside, Liddy was checking all the windows and doors, and Jet stood on the parlour windowsill, staring out into the darkness.

"Draw every shutter, blind and curtain, Liddy, please, apart from the one in your bedroom and we shall watch out of there. I will carry Jet up and he'll be safe with us."

"Must he come, Miss? I mean, couldn't we leave him down here?"

"No Liddy, we couldn't. He may get frightened on his own and besides, he has been through hell in his life so far."

Liddy replied that he was far more likely to frighten them with the bad luck he brought.

"Rubbish," vented Verity, thoroughly vexed, "I told you, I will not hear any more of your nonsense but you may stay down here on your own if you dislike his company so much."

Half an hour later, all three were in Liddy's room, and Jet made himself comfortable on the bed. Liddy was secretly horrified but kept that to herself.

Verity regarded him with affection.

"He is very much at ease at present, so nothing will happen for now but watch him, as he will tell us when one of those creatures draws near."

"Friends of his," Liddy muttered, under her breath.

"Cats are very sensitive to atmospheres and they know when folk are against them. They feel the negative vibrations so, if you persist in airing your views in front of him, then you and I will part company!" the mistress warned her maid, "Jet will be our eyes and ears tonight. He repels evil, he does not attract it. All cats are precious gifts from the divine."

Liddy pursed up her lips but never said a word.

All was quiet until about 2am, when Jet suddenly became very restless. He got up, climbed on the windowsill and looking out into the darkness, began to hiss. His tail was huge and, when he spotted something in the garden, he snarled and growled, as if in warning.

"What has he seen?" cried Verity, jumping to attention. It was impossible to keep the fear out of her voice.

"I can't see anything," replied Liddy, peering out into the darkness.

Verity scanned the garden and then pointed with a shaking finger.

"There," she whispered. "Look..."

Liddy did so and could just make out two creeping figures traversing the path and stopping frequently to smell the trail of blood.

"They are bending down now and one of them is on her knees...I say 'her' for it seems to be a woman."

"Yes, both of them appear female," Liddy told her, "And they are approaching the shed. Oh, I pray that the men have seen them and are ready. Are they vampires, do you think?"

A sudden shaft of moonlight lit up the garden and illuminated the faces of the young women who had tangled, black hair and pale, twisted faces. Their eyes were cadaverous and black, and Liddy drew back from the window in fear. Verity prayed silently that both Frederick and Lawrence were prepared.

In the shed, Frederick gripped his Bible tighter. "They have found us," he whispered to Lawrence, "Hark! They come closer."

"I am ready," Lawrence said, quietly but with conviction, "When they get to the shed door, I will throw it open and flash the lantern upon them," he raised the light and began to fumble with the slats, "When the light hits them, they will recoil in horror and it will delay their progress so, to weaken them further, I will throw the Holy Water upon them, which burns like fire and that will leave you free to strike!"

"I shall send in the love vibration first," murmured Frederick, his throat drying up with anticipation, "It seems to be the two women I followed from the crossroads, a few weeks back. Hopefully they should be easy to overpower."

One of the women had reached the bucket of blood and she gave a cry of delight and began to drink from it, spilling a great deal in her haste to consume the life force.

"Now!" cried Lawrence, "Before they drink too much and rekindle their power. Hopefully they will not have fed for a day or so! Quick, and we can dispatch them before they digest the blood!"

He kicked the shed door open and thrust the lantern in the women's faces. They both screamed as the light hit them and drew back, so that Lawrence was able to follow them and scatter the Holy Water over their pale faces. He caught a whiff of their stale, fetid breath and the smell made him nauseous but he carried on until the container was empty. The women screamed as the water burnt their skins and blurred their sight and Frederick, taking advantage of this, leapt out with his Bible and crucifix in front of him. One of the women made as if to jump on him, but he thrust the cross in her face, and she whimpered and leapt back.

"And may the love of God, which passes all understanding, surround you both with its bright, eternal light and may that refulgence enter your body and travel down from your head to your toes, illuminating every organ as it passes through, driving out evil." The women writhed in agony and Frederick thought they were home and dry but the one who had drunk the blood seemed to recover a little and leapt into the air, twisting as she went. Lawrence looked on in dismay as she changed rapidly into a bat and, flapping her wings, soared over their heads and away.

The other woman was weaker and more of the water had burnt her, so she huddled on the floor screaming for help from the creatures of the night.

"Hurry! Hurry!" cried Lawrence, "Or she too may transform into an animal and elude us. Quick – the stake and mallet!"

Frederick stepped forward and both those weapons were in his hand.

"May the love of God take you!" he cried, before taking his aim,

"May God forgive me for what I am going to do, and may the Devil pass out of this woman and the hosts of God get ready to receive her!"

The woman, though weak, tried to bite Frederick and it took both of them to subdue her and fling her onto her back but still she fought and kicked, and the spittle ran from her mouth onto the earth and sizzled as it met the dry soil. But Frederick's aim was practised and before long, he raised the stake and impaled her, catching the heart straight away and driving it in with the mallet.

A massive sigh convulsed the woman, the blood ran from her and turned to green liquid, and Lawrence stood, praying over her, as she breathed her last.

"Bless you, bless you. No more pain and no more eternal wanderings to find blood. May you find the love of Christ."

The woman writhed once more and then, a smile of peace transfixed her face and she was suddenly still.

To Verity, watching from the window, every second seemed like an eternity and the tension was heightened by the fact that she could see little of what was going on. Liddy, however, possessed excellent night vision and she missed

66

nothing. The moonlight was being elusive but when the lantern came out in Lawrence's hand, both the women could see the vampire lunging at the men.

"Oh, be careful Frederick," murmured Verity under her breath, her whisper harsh with anxiety. Darkness descended again, and when the moon finally broke free from her nest of clouds and showed the creature trying to attack Frederick again, Verity could take no more. She turned from the window and declared she could not watch.

Cuddling Jet to her heart, she sat on the bed and tried to lose herself in his rhythmic purr.

"Convey to me what is happening, Liddy, please but only the good...I can't bear the bad!"

Liddy's sharp eyes missed very little and she kept up a running commentary to her mistress who, alternately, despaired and hoped.

"And one of the women, the one who drank the blood and got strong, has turned herself into a giant bat! Yes, she has escaped, Miss, Yes, there she goes over the house front."

"And there is no sign of my uncle at all?"

"No, Miss, just the two women, who could be the ones Mr Frederick followed back to this very house. Ah, they have the other one and it looks like they mean to dispatch her!"

"Oh, Liddy, that is awful!"

"She'd be for biting Mr Frederick, for sure, and passing on her affliction, Miss!"

"Oh, yes, of course. No, not terrible at all then."

"He has the stake ready, Miss, and the mallet raised!"

"No more, Liddy, or I shall be sick, and Jet is shaking, I am sure he is. Just tell me when it is all over," And she buried her face in Jet's well-groomed fur.

A slow minute went by.

"Well?" asked Verity, unable to bear the suspense any longer.

"She's gone, Miss. To heaven, I hope."

Verity stood up.

"Sit here with Jet as I must see Frederick," and gleaning a handful of burnished twigs from a vase, some with blood-red berries on them, she left the room.

Jet sat up and fixed his beady eyes on Liddy. The maid could not help smiling at him.

"I guess you're not too bad for a black one, and maybe you did bring us some luck tonight," she told the cat, "One down anyway and one to go, unless of course you helped that one get away?"

Jet shook his head at this and scratched an ear.

Liddy put her hand out and solemnly the cat raised a paw. "Friends," said Liddy, and together the cat and maid approached the window to see what their mistress was up to.

Verity turned the heavy, old key in the back door and pushed open the barrier, feeling the cold, night air rushing in upon her. Her head felt feverish and yet her teeth chattered with cold. The dark enveloped her but the smell of blood was still sharp upon the air and she followed it and struck the path to the shed.

"Frederick! Frederick!" she called.

The tall figure standing over the prostrate body straightened up and stared in disbelief. Whatever happened, Verity must not see this, he thought.

Lawrence saw his friend's tense features and called out, "Stay back, Miss!"

Verity, however, had no intention of returning tamely to the house and she came resolutely onwards. She saw the dark flowing hair, almost the same hue as hers, the closed eyes and the alabaster skin, and empathy for a fellow human enveloped her soul. She swallowed a sob and knelt down by the woman, ignoring Frederick's hand which he extended towards her. The young woman looked as if she had fallen asleep and Verity began to adorn her head with the twigs she carried, pushing them gently into the silken locks, and arranging them around her neck. Frederick looked on in sorrow and he felt tears bead his dark lashes. He knelt down

68

beside Verity and tried to take her hand in his but she eluded him and half turned away.

"She's gone, Verity. She's gone."

They were simple words, said with a hint of remorse and Verity felt the tears flowing. She gazed up at Frederick and found he too, was crying.

"I had to do it," he breathed, in a soothing tone, "I had no choice, once she was bitten..."

"Once, she was just like me," murmured Verity to herself, as though the man's words had not reached her. She stroked the long hair gently, "We could almost be sisters," she continued.

"I sent her to heaven, you know. Before that, she was in hell," Frederick told her and this time, to his relief, she nodded whilst the tears flowed.

Verity stood up.

"Can we pray for her?" she asked, in a low voice, "She looks so beautiful now."

"She was a screaming, lusting harpy, consumed by the desire for blood, and set to wander the world for eternity but God has seen fit to restore her earthly beauty," put in Lawrence.

"And do you know her?" asked Verity, staring at Lawrence so he felt awkward and could not frame a lie.

"I do," he said.

"And who is she?"

"Rose Malkin. She disappeared a few weeks ago and we feared the worst then."

"Was she a good girl before...before the bite came upon her?"

"Yes, Miss, she was a teacher at the local school. Well, she had only been there a year but the children liked her well enough."

Verity shook her head.

"What a waste," she intoned. She took a deep breath.

"Pray with me," she continued, holding out her hands to the men.

They joined hands over the body and Verity said simply,

"Into your merciful hands, Oh Lord, we commend this Rose. True, the petals have faded and the bud will open on this world no more but, please, let her soul be blameless and pure when she attains the gates of Heaven. Please, St Peter, let her in, for she knew not what she did and we must all show her compassion. Amen."

It was late afternoon the same day and Frederick and Lawrence had gone, taking the body with them. There was to be a funeral in two days time and the story that was put into circulation was that the men had come upon the body, whilst out walking. It saved the grieving parent the horror of knowing what the daughter had become but a few knew the truth, or guessed it, and many a nod or wink occured when it was spoken of in the village.

Liddy had slept like a baby and only Verity had remained wakeful. Jet had snored on the bottom of his mistress's bed, ignoring the tossing and turning of the occupant, for cats really can sleep through a visitation from hell when they are tired.

And how many more of them are out there, wondered Verity, as she sat by the fire, with a sad expression on her wan features? She heard Liddy preparing tea and singing to herself, and though she was glad that the maid had changed her attitude to her dear friend, yet her heart remained heavy. She leant her hot forehead against the glass and heard the grating ring as the gate moved outside. Dusk had come, slow but sure, and she could not see who was there but Liddy went to answer the knock, drying her hands as she did so.

Verity heard a woman's voice in the hallway and presently, Liddy knocked at the door, reluctant to disturb her mistress but knowing the visitor waited for an answer.

"Yes Liddy," called out Verity, returning to the fire.

Liddy came in awkwardly, not meeting Verity's eye, as she knew her mistress was still very upset and had not slept much.

"It's...it's Mrs Malkin to see you, Miss. I told her you were indisposed but she insisted."

Rose's mother! Verity felt a surge of panic. What did she want with me? she thought.

"You don't have to see her, Miss, I can send her away."

"And she will only come back, won't she, Liddy?"

"Yes, Miss, I believe she will."

"Wouldn't you if it was your daughter found…found dead?"

"I suppose so, Miss. What am I to say then?"

Verity gave a great sigh.

"Say I will see her briefly and show her in, Liddy, and some tea and cakes would thaw the ice a little, I hope."

"Yes, Miss, of course."

CHAPTER SIX

Verity remained standing by the fire. She had no idea what she was going to say or do. Her heart went out to the woman but her soul was numb after last night. Whatever happened the secret had to be kept, as to betray both Frederick and Lawrence was not an option. If more people knew exactly what was happening under their nose, as such, mass panic would ensue and then,0 how was Frederick to track down the other vampire? And there must be more.

She wondered what story Mrs Malkin had been told, and by whom, and she knew she had to summon all her wits if she were to get out of this without revealing the truth. Last night's work had to remain as silent as the grave.

Verity heard a sound behind her and turned, coming face to face with Rose's mother who stood awkwardly by the door. She cleared her throat.

"Mrs Malkin. Let me begin by saying how sorry I am for your tragic loss. I believe the girl had been missing for a while?" She tried to keep her eyes on Mrs Malkin's steely blue eyes, but her heart raced and she felt vaguely sick. The woman was an older copy of the daughter for sure.

"She had...yes. Just suddenly left her lodgings. She wanted her independence, you see, and left one dark, cold night and was never seen again. Then suddenly, she turns up dead on your doorstep."

"Is that what you have been told?" enquired Verity, trying to keep calm. "Please do sit down, Mrs Malkin, as it feels very formal with us both standing."

"I'll not say I won't be glad to, Miss Whittle."

"Verity, please. I do not stand on ceremony, everyone calls me Verity, apart from Liddy, and she prefers Miss."

"I heard Mr Frederick was familiar enough to do that too."

Verity broke her gaze and regarded her feet. Where was this leading?

"And was it Mr Frederick who told you your daughter's body was found here?"

"No, it was Mr Lawrence who called."

"Ah...I see."

"So Mr Frederick was involved too was he?" Mrs Malkin retorted, sharply, "I have heard what sort of man he is."

"Really? And what sort of man is that, may I ask?"

"Rumours spread, Verity, as I am sure you are aware."

"They do, indeed, but they are not always composed of the truth, are they?"

"I think this one contains at least a grain of it."

"Then perhaps you would enlighten me, Mrs Malkin, as I have lately come to this place and have not had opportunity to go into the village, as yet."

"Well, they say Mr Frederick frequents this house all times of the day and night. In short, he stays over."

"And are you concerned for my honour? For my good name?"

"I don't care a fig for that, miss, to be honest but I want to find out what happened to my daughter.

Mr Lawrence said she was found here by yourself, when you were out searching for your errant cat last night."

"Did he?" replied Verity, "Well, yes, that is so, and did he also tell you I screamed for Liddy to wake her up? Then I sent her off in search of Mr Frederick and Mr Lawrence, they being the only people I am acquainted with in the village."

"Acquainted is a good word, miss."

"Would you like me to use another word then? Say that they are both my friends, maybe?"

"Happen, and one of them closer than that and we all know which one that is, of course."

Verity got up. She was becoming increasingly angry.

"Mrs Malkin, it seems you have come here to cross question me as to the truth of the so-called rumours that are circulating round the village. Is that not so?"

The widow had the grace to look abashed.

"I am sorry if you see it that way but truth will out, you know. Of course, I have come about my daughter but they do say..."

"Mrs Malkin, I will say it again that I do not tolerate having gossip repeated. I said the same to my maid only a few hours ago. If you persist in this, then I shall have no option but to ask you to leave."

A dangerously, icy silence fell. Verity felt she was holding her own against this tyrant of a woman.

"It is what they say Mr Frederick is that concerns me, miss."

"Really? And what is that?"

"A vampire hunter."

Verity turned away as the words came tumbling out. Composing herself, she came and sat down again.

"It is common talk that we have vampires here, ripping the sheep up and drinking their blood," continued Mrs Malkin.

"Perhaps a lone wolf, or a mad dog, or a pack of them?"

"Possibly, but there has also been talk of your uncle being one of them."

"What? A dog?"

"No, miss, a vampire. You must have heard such things yourself, as he was your flesh and blood, as it were!"

"I don't listen to gossip, Mrs Malkin, and I suggest you don't either. Stick to facts. My uncle was dead long before I came here."

"Ah...but was he? Why did Mr Frederick come here and profess such an interest in him and this house? More importantly, how come it was those men who were called to see my daughter's body last night?"

"I told you that they are the only two people I know here." Verity stroked her dress as she spoke, as if to try and calm her racing mind.

"Bit of a coincidence don't you think, seeing as Mr Frederick came on purpose of chasing vampires and you finding my Rose and summoning him. Why not the priest? Or the doctor?"

"I am not acquainted with either of those gentlemen. I simply called Mr Frederick as a friend in my hour of need. It was a terrible shock to find her."

"And was she...was she..."

"Yes, she was dead when I found her."

74

"But the doctor could not find a mark on her?"

"No? And did he say what she died of?"

"He was mystified when I saw him."

"Did Mr Frederick know?"

"Did you let him examine the body, miss?"

"Yes...well, I was in a state and came inside and left the two gentlemen to move the body. Sorry, I mean your precious daughter."

"Did Mr Lawrence know who she was? Did he recognise her like that?"

"Yes, he did, but details of last night are a bit vague with the lingering shock."

"He knows me very well and he watched Rose grow up, of course. He helped us when I lost my husband - Rose's father. I had a baby on the way but the shock meant I lost it."

"I am so sorry."

"I have high regard for Mr Grey. I was not happy when I heard that he was in the company of the vampire hunter, I can tell you."

Verity felt they were going round in circles.

"That is rumour, Mrs Malkin, and I tell you I won't listen to it."

The door opened at this point and Liddy came in with the tea tray. Verity was glad for the diversion and she tried to pour with a steady hand. She knew Liddy would tell by her face that she was struggling.

Mrs Malkin accepted some tea with a nod and, after a quick mouthful, she said, in a more compliant tone,

"I have to know, miss. You know exactly what I am going to ask you."

Verity let her eyes fall to her cup. She noticed her hands were shaking.

"I think so," she murmured.

"Please, please, tell me if you know anything more, no matter how trivial. Anything at all that links my daughter to the mystery killing of sheep or this vampire hunter coming. In other words, Miss Whittle, was my daughter killed by one of those bloodsuckers?"

Worded like that, Verity told herself her mouth was not framing a lie.

"No, Mrs Malkin," she said, with some conviction, "She was not. You have my word on that."

It was two hours later and Verity was feeling more composed. She had sent Liddy with a note to Frederick's lodgings, asking him to come and see her as soon as possible.

Mrs Malkin had departed soon after drinking her tea and for that Verity was very grateful. But as she left, she grabbed Verity's hand, stared deep into her eyes and pleaded with her to attend the funeral, seeing as she found Rose.

"Should anything else come back to you, or your conscience prick you, then your maid knows where I live," she had shot, as her parting comment.

"My conscience, Mrs Malkin, is clear," Verity had replied to her visitor's back. "I found a dead girl and have done my duty by restoring her to her loving family."

Mrs Malkin did not reply and Verity heard her leave a minute later, without another word. Liddy came in at once to take the tray and stood gazing at her mistress. Verity got up and, walking over to the fire, warmed her cold hands.

"Liddy, you may look at me until supper time but I am not going to tell you what was said. I need you to take a note to Mr Frederick for me."

"Very well, miss. I was only going to comment that Mrs Malkin left in quite a mood and grabbed the door out of my hand and slammed it."

"Well, she had her reasons. Now, leave me please to write this note and once you have washed up the tea cups be so good as to do my bidding."

Liddy pursed up her mouth but she knew her mistress was aware she had heard a large proportion of the conversation by listening at the parlour door.

A few hours after Liddy delivered the message, Verity heard Frederick's knock at the door and saw his tall form from the parlour window. Liddy admitted him without a word, and Verity knew she was sulking about her mistress's silence concerning her visitor. Nevertheless, once Frederick was in, Verity bade him warm his hands by the fire and checked outside the door, where she knew Liddy frequently hid. The hallway was empty and she heard her maid taking out her temper on the pots and pans in the kitchen.

"Liddy," said her mistress, in a loud clear voice – by way of explanation- "listens in on my conversations."

"You wish to talk to me on private matters then?" asked her guest.

Verity nodded.

"Gossip is lifeblood to Liddy, I am afraid, and I do not want things said in this parlour to be repeated in the village."

"That sounds serious."

"It is," responded Verity, lowering her voice now, "Frederick, Mrs Malkin came to see me."

"Ah, now I understand the secrecy," He raised his eyebrows and light dawned in his dark eyes.

"What happened?" he continued, turning from the fire.

Verity clasped and unclasped her hands. She still felt upset when she thought about her guest.

"I had to lie to her, or to be strictly honest, I covered up the truth, but couldn't you have warned me?"

Frederick came closer and took her hand.

"I am so sorry," he murmured, "We had no idea she would do that. As Lawrence knew the family, it seemed easier for him to inform her mother what had happened. I never thought of Mrs Malkin coming here. I expected her to be grieving over the corpse at the undertakers."

"She came straight here, it seems, to cross question me and, of course, I did not know what had passed between you all. I managed to glean from her that Lawrence went to see her but she inferred things about us, Frederick, and I do not like to be the subject of gossip. Why, I have only been here for a few days and look, I am causing a stir in the village!"

"That will pass," replied Frederick, "And bigger and juicier pieces of scandal will replace you."

"So you think I am a scandal then?"

Frederick laughed but would not be drawn.

"How did it finish with Mrs Malkin?" he enquired.

"She is suspicious, that I am sure of, but she has no proof. I told her I do not give gossip house room and reminded her that I had been here no time at all."

"Obviously long enough to get a bad name, in that lady's eyes!"

"I think she knows that there is some connection with her daughter's death and the vampires frequenting the area. I played things very cool but she wasn't fooled and I fear we have not seen the last of her. Why, she even asked me to go to the funeral but I expect that was only so she could interrogate me further."

"You are considering going?"

"I fear it will look very suspicious if I don't."

"Well, Lawrence will go, of course, being connected with the family, so he could take you and look after you."

"You won't attend then?"

"I think I need to keep in the shadows after last night. Clearly, that will not be possible for long as we still have the other woman, your uncle and possibly a master to track down before we can all sleep easy in our beds."

"So you will watch again tonight?"

"The woman will not be back, that is for sure. Your uncle? Well, he might but I think I need to cast the net wider. I could transport the vats of blood in a cart and try the moorland road after midnight."

"But won't someone see you?"

"Few go that way after dark. I will be gone by first light, which is not until 8 in the morning in January. That may prove fruitful. However, I think I will leave it until this funeral is over."

"I fear for your safety, Frederick, in those rough, wild parts."

"As long as we have our protection and each other, we will be safe, dear lady, so do not fear. I heard only today that I am needed in the wilds of Wales, where a group of vampires are preying on village children and slaughtering them, much as we kill cattle for beef."

"With the bloodlust so strong in them, that is the way vampires think of them, doubtlessly," replied Verity but her heart sank and her voice was faltering, she noticed. Frederick going! Discussing his plans for the future with her as calmly as he had with Lawrence, no doubt.

"You will miss Lawrence," she continued, when silence had reigned for a moment or two. Her voice was still not her own but Frederick did not appear to notice. Overcome with emotion, she bent to put more wood on the fire, in order to hide the tears in her eyes.

"I will return to visit him," Frederick told her, "I criss-cross the country since these creatures chose our isles to make their home, so he will never be far away. He may yet, of course, decide to come with me but if he retires I hope he will be a reliable friend for you, when I am gone."

He says it so lightly and without a care, thought Verity and suddenly, all the joy had gone out of the day.

"But you'll not go until the vampires here are destroyed?"

"No, I'll finish my job first," he replied.

"So will you go out tonight, when you know the eyes and the ears of the village are alert, watching and listening, after Rose's death?"

"No, I stick to what I said earlier. I will wait until the funeral is over and things have quietened down."

"Sorry," Verity murmured, "Of course you told me when you first came in. I don't quite know what is wrong with me today. Shall I ring for some tea?"

"No, pray do not trouble yourself or Liddy. If you have accepted my heartfelt apology for involving you in an unpleasant situation, I'll be on my way."

"It was far more than just unpleasant, Frederick. 'Unpleasant' describes burnt porridge for breakfast or cold soup for dinner."

"We were careless but we were tired, and in some shock, for, even after years of doing this work, well, Verity, I am still a murderer fifty times over and I carry on killing. Yes,

Lawrence was thinking of retiring from this line of work, as he has taken it hard, but he did not strike the final blow."

"You think he'll continue to do this job then, for a while longer? Will he come away with you when you go?"

"He has ties in this area that make it more difficult for him to leave...."

"But not impossible?"

"No."

There was a brief silence and Frederick rose to go. Verity was hit by a rash notion.

"What if there were three of you at the crossroads, watching and waiting, for the bloodsuckers to come?"

Frederick looked confused.

"I will not share this secret with anyone, be they outside the village or not," he told Verity firmly.

"But what if they already knew the state of things?"

Again, Frederick looked puzzled.

"I have told no-one," he replied, "And you?"

A sudden light dawned in his eye.

"You?" he cried, "You?"

"Why not? I could run for help, should it be needed."

"No, it is crazy. I will not have you exposed to danger."

"But it is not your choice! I am an adult...I am a..."

"You are a woman and a very fragile one too," interrupted Frederick.

"But it is MY uncle who is draining the village of blood!"

Frederick laughed.

"What is this, Verity?" he asked. "Some sort of penance for his sins? Are you mad?"

"Possibly," she said, evenly. "Maybe it runs in the family."

"I cannot allow it," continued Frederick, "If Lawrence were here, he would say the same."

"Do you know that for sure? Have you asked him?"

Frederick shook his head.

"The thought of you helping us and becoming exposed to danger has never, ever entered my head. Stay here and keep the doors locked."

"So what if I walk out to the crossroads when you are there?"

"Then I would have to bring you back and, in doing so, I would leave Lawrence alone, and so expose him to even more danger!"

"Then let me come with you at the start and then you can bring me home together, when we have dispatched these devils!"

"Never."

"You are a very infuriating man, Frederick."

"You are a very foolish, young woman, Verity."

"Think about it, please," she responded, in a softer tone. Frederick looked at her and saw she was in deadly earnest. She was so persuasive, and her beauty so heightened, when she was aflame with passion.

He regained control of himself, with difficulty.

"It cannot be," he said simply, kissed her hand and, fearing he was weakening, he left.

To say Verity was vexed by Frederick's instant dismissal of her plan was, indeed, an understatement. When Liddy came in to ask about dinner, her mistress was still clearly agitated. Walking up and down and shaking her head, muttering to herself, "How dare he? How dare he?" did nothing to calm her mood either.

"Are you quite well, miss?" asked Liddy, with concern, "For I would say you seem very distracted. There's me enquired three times now as to the time for dinner and you appear not to have heard at all!"

Verity stopped her perambulating and stared at her maid, as if seeing her for the first time. Liddy felt uncomfortable under such steely eyes.

"What if I asked you to accompany me to the crossroads, at midnight, to assist Mr Frederick and Mr Lawrence in vampire hunting, Liddy?"

Liddy felt even more awkward but the idea did not appeal to her at all.

"I'd say I'd rather not do it, miss, if you don't mind. I am sure two such formidable gentlemen can cope on their own!"

"But what if I ordered you to do it?"

"As part of my duties you mean?"

"Yes."

"Well, then I'd have to." She thought for a minute and then replied, as an afterthought,

"I still say I'd rather not, miss."

"Have you no sense of adventure, Liddy?"

"My common sense tells me to remain in bed at night, miss," replied Liddy, "If Mr Frederick told you the same thing, as I am sure he did, I suggest you take his advice. Happen you might not listen to ME, a lowly maid, but HE is far higher in your heart, I am sure!" and, so saying, she flounced out of the room.

"I seem to have upset Liddy somehow."

It was three days later and Frederick had arrived to talk about the funeral. Verity felt there was an atmosphere between them after her last outburst and she was determined to dispel it.

Frederick put his empty cup back on the tray and raised his eyebrows.

"How?" he asked.

Verity filled his cup and handed him the plate of cakes.

"The way I upset everyone and the way I upset YOU, last time we met."

Frederick stirred his tea.

"You didn't upset me," he replied, quietly, "You just came up with a very dangerous idea, that is all."

"Well, I enlightened Liddy on my idea and suggested she came with me to the crossroads when you were vampire hunting!"

"Oh, I see, so two women's safety would be put at risk."

Verity flushed.

"She...she wasn't happy at all, especially since I said I might order her to do it."

Frederick raised his eyebrows again.

"Are you sure she hasn't put salt instead of sugar in the cakes?"

"She wouldn't do that, as she knows you eat more of them than me. She has been very sharp and curt with me for the last couple of days and I don't like it."

"Have you told Liddy you have completely let go of the idea of travelling at midnight to the crossroads?"

"No, not exactly."

"Because you haven't," finished Frederick, reaching for another cake,

"Well, these taste fine and up to Liddy's usual high standard. Her mother is a good cook, too."

"Don't change the subject, Frederick."

"I am afraid I must, Verity, as I need to talk about the funeral arrangements and then depart. Another sheep has been found dead and bloodless."

"So, when will you start at the crossroads?" asked Verity, not entirely giving up her idea on accompanying him.

"Next week I think. I don't believe we can leave it any longer. Animals are still being mutilated, every night. I hope you keep that cat of yours in after dark."

"Of course," replied Verity, in horror of anything happening to her darling.

"Where is he, by the way?"

"Asleep on Liddy's bed when I last looked."

"She doesn't mind?"

"No, she seems to have quite accepted him."

"But not the mad plan to go out to the crossroads at midnight?"

"No."

  Frederick put his plate down and dusted a few crumbs off his trousers.

"I appreciate very much what you are trying to do for me," he said gently, looking at Verity, "I am sorry but it will cause more trouble than it is worth."

"How?"

"I am not going through all that again."

"In case you weaken?"

83

"Not at all. Lawrence agrees with me. You cannot put your life in danger."

"But you endanger yours?"

"I am a man and, besides, that is my job. Now, let us say no more on the subject and move on to the funeral. You still intend going?"

"Yes, I think I should. I am not going to give Mrs Malkin the satisfaction that she has frightened me off. She asked me but it was almost a dare."

Frederick nodded.

"Well, you will have Lawrence with you, and I have told him not to leave your side."

"A white knight, eh?"

"Lawrence knows the family well, so I trust his presence there with you will soothe any ire and turn away any anger."

"Well, it will not come from ME," promised Verity.

"Lawrence will pick you up at 1 o'clock and, as soon as is decent, he will escort you home. There should be no need for you to stay out after darkness. In fact, I think most of the mourners will want to be safely home by then."

"People know what is happening then?"

"I would say they suspect rather than know. At least, that is what I hope."

"I hope so too."

A pregnant silence reigned, then both began to speak at once.

Verity smiled.

"Sorry," she said, "You first."

"I was just going to say, I have to go." He got up.

"Make your peace with Liddy," he said, by means of goodbye, "We have enemies enough without upsetting those near and dear."

Verity rose as well.

"I haven't upset you?" she enquired.

Frederick pulled on his gloves but shook his head.

"You never could, my dear lady," he said, and kissed her hand. She heard Liddy let him out and his footsteps fade on the path. She sighed and went to assume the role of peacemaker.

CHAPTER SEVEN

"Do you want me to brush your hair any particular way, miss?" asked Liddy, pausing with her comb arrested over Verity's hair. It was two days later and the morning of the funeral.

Verity regarded herself in the mirror. She looked tired and strained and there were dark shadows under her eyes. She had not slept well the past couple of nights and she struggled with food and drink.

"That's a comb, Liddy."

"Well, miss, you know what I mean. My aunt taught me how to style hair when I was young and now I do my own tresses." She patted her neat bun.

"Up I think, please," replied her mistress, scooping her dark locks in one hand and piling them on top of her head, "I want to look taller and more austere, I think."

"To frighten Mrs Malkin off?"

"No, Liddy, just to make her leave me alone."

"You have lost flesh and vitality since you came here?"

"Yes. It is this business with the vampires. I cannot rest at night and my mind churns..."

"Ah, you fear for Mr Frederick's life, now you know he means to be at the crossroads next week. THAT is why you want to accompany him."

"Now, now, Liddy, you'll have us romantically linked next. I apologised for my mad idea but how can I sleep when I know he is out there?"

"He does it for a living, miss. It is his choice. He has Mr Lawrence with him."

"So, you have no fears for either of them then?"

"None that will disturb my sleep, miss. They will be in my prayers every night, that is for sure, and I will send them love and the protection of Michael's cloak, too."

"Michael?"

"Archangel Michael, miss. My mother was always asking him for protection when we were far from her. I will bind his silver and blue cloak round both of them."

"Mind you do then, Liddy, and do not forget one single night!"

Verity stood up and the simple, black dress fell about her gaunt form.

"There now, I am ready and just await Mr Lawrence. Will I do, Liddy?"

"Very presentable, miss."

"I want to get lost in the crowd, as it were. I want to blend in. Tell me what sort of girl Rose was. Did you know her?"

"Yes, miss, she was very steady. No sweetheart that we knew of, and just lived for her job, helping children."

"What about her family?"

"Mr Lawrence knows them better than me, miss. You should ask him."

"Her father is dead, I understand, and she did not live with her mother."

"No, miss, I believe there was a disagreement when her father died, over the money he left."

"Yet her mother sees fit to accuse ME of wrongdoing concerning her daughter's death."

"Guilt bites deep, miss. It was said Mrs Malkin had not spoken to Rose since she left the house to train for her position."

"So, was that long ago?"

"Two years – perhaps three. Rose was older than me, so we did not have the same friends in the village. All I really knew about her was how quiet and secretive she appeared, even when you met her, she rarely said much."

"So, you think she and her mother were estranged at the time of her death?"

"I believe so, but Mr Lawrence would confirm this. It was said it was a full week before Mrs Malkin knew her daughter was missing, Rose's landlady being aware of the rift and so not informing her mother at first. I bet she regretted it though, as I heard Mrs Malkin went to see her when it all came out and made free with her tongue."

Verity smiled.

"Yes," she nodded, "I can imagine that."

"Go easy on her today, miss, as grief makes us say things we come to regret later, and once words are uttered, they cannot be unsaid."

"Never fear, Liddy, as I shall leave the talking to Lawrence, so he can defend my honour."

Liddy gave a knowing look but, as Verity was taking a last glance in the mirror, she missed it. A few minutes later, Mr Lawrence was announced by Liddy.

"Ah Lawrence – nice to see you again," Verity told him, "Come into the parlour and warm up before we leave, as the wind is bitter today. Liddy went to the village earlier and came back shivering with chattering teeth!"

"It is indeed, very cold," replied Lawrence, removing his gloves before the genial blaze, "A day not fit for man nor beast to be out, and not a day to lay poor Rose to rest at all."

"But will she rest this time, Lawrence? Will she really lie in the sod and not rise up again to stalk us all?"

"The bloodlust is over for her, Miss Whittle, at last. Think no more of that, for she sits on a cloud and gazes down at us, I believe. She knows there was no other way we could help her, besides what we did. A deep peace has entered her soul and may it never leave."

The church was freezing cold, and a number of people were already there, although Lawrence and Verity were early. She held his arm and walked to a pew with her head held high but the embarrassment caused her to pale and feel slightly sick. Of course, every head was turned her way and their eyes were on her, the stranger in the village, the person shrouded in mystery who had taken over her uncle's house, knowing full well the rumours that circulated. She felt a twinge of guilt for the lies she had told but the truth would have been impossible to reveal. The damage it would do to both Frederick and Lawrence! She gripped her companion's arm and wished the eyes would leave her shaking form.

"I feel I am in a zoo," she whispered to Lawrence, when she heard more footsteps ringing out on stone and attention was off her a little. "Some are still staring."

Lawrence smiled.

"That is village life for you," he replied, calmly, "They look because you are a stranger and have not walked among them. Many are the questions I have had to answer about you. 'Do you know Miss Whittle? What sort of woman is she?' Every day too, in my dealings in the village, the questions have come thick and fast."

"I hope you have replied favourably," whispered Verity.

"Well, Miss Whittle, I have only been acquainted with you lately. I would say Frederick knows you better but I have, of course, replied you are a woman of class and character and one likely to do the village good."

"Thank you, Lawrence, I knew I could rely on you."

Rose's family entered now and walked up to the front pew but Verity could feel the daggers at her heart, from the blazing looks she received. It appeared there was a younger sister and a tall man, who could have been Mrs Malkin's brother, so great was the resemblance. The quiet burr of conversation ended, silence descended on the congregation and the priest stood up to speak.

'God, give me the strength to get through this,' thought Verity, steeling her spirits and trying to hold her head up high.

They were at the graveside now, and the wind and showers of January blew in upon them. The long, slow, sad words of the service rained down on the huddled souls, some quietly crying, others bowing their heads in mutual respect. The mourners were silent as the priest chanted,

"Ashes to ashes, dust to dust."

Verity felt her eyes bead with tears and she kept her head low. Lawrence seemed immersed in his own world. She wondered if the man was thinking of the hellish task that he and Frederick faced.

The flowers were thrown down. "A rose for a Rose," murmured Mrs Malkin. Then the earth descended with a dull thud onto the simple wooden coffin and hail made all the petals sparkle. The priest closed his book and, wishing everyone well with his handshakes, he departed.

Across the grave, Verity faced Mrs Malkin's keen eye. Now that the service was over, that lady was awake again, no longer immured in the doctrine of the moment and out for revenge. Despite having hold of her younger daughter's hand, her mind and lips were ready for action.

"Everyone is welcome at the funeral tea, apart from a certain lady, who knows who she is and what she has done," she began, when she had checked the priest was out of earshot, "In short, she is banned from the house."

"Hush, Lavinia," from Lawrence, holding up his hand for peace, "Today is not the day for throwing unfounded accusations, please think of Rose and honour her memory."

"Seeing as you take her arm and remain by her side, Lawrence, you will not sup with us either. Until you come to your senses and see what a...a witch you have taken under your wing, you are not welcome in our home any longer. There is another in your company who has also been bewitched by her spells. Everyone here knows of whom I speak."

Verity shrank back from the eyes of the crowd. Why, they were all staring and now Mrs Malkin was slurring Frederick too! She felt like picking up her skirts and running away. Turning, she began to creep away but a sudden noise behind her made her stop, and looking nervously over her shoulder, she saw her adversary had followed her.

"Ah, yes, creep away like the toad that you are," the widow began. Verity turned to desperately try and calm the situation. The anger and hatred were getting out of hand.

"Mrs Malkin and everyone here, let me assure you that I know no more about your daughter's death than you do. I found her and that is all."

"What was she doing up at your place, anyway?" retorted the woman, sharply, "What caused her death there and, in short, what did you do to her?"

"I did nothing, Mrs Malkin, as I told you when you called upon me. I didn't even know who she was or that she was missing. I only learnt that later from Lawrence."

"Ah, yes, try to blame him. It was Frederick you called, of course, and he has covered your misdemeanours with a cloak of silence. Both gentlemen are utterly in your power, it seems."

"They would not lie for me!" Verity almost shouted, furious to hear Frederick's name twisted with her own by this tyrant.

In answer to that, Mrs Malkin leapt forward and grabbed Verity's arm. Twisting it cruelly in her strong grasp, she shouted in Verity's face,

"You know more than you are letting on! You know how she died and of what. You may have hidden it for now, but the truth WILL surface!"

Suddenly Lawrence was there, pulling the widow off Verity and standing between them.

Verity rubbed her arm which was painful and throbbing. "Lavinia, please! This is not the place to conduct an argument. This lady knows nothing anyway, I swear..."

"Lady, eh? I don't think so."

Lawrence took Verity's uninjured arm and they drew off but Mrs Malkin shouted after them,

"I'll be here, waiting for when you come to your senses and tell the truth! Do you hear? It won't stay hidden forever! You know how my daughter died, you and your uncle! Wasn't there talk of him enticing young girls to his place? What did he do there, Miss Whittle? What did he do?"

Lawrence could not let that go unanswered. He turned furiously.

"You know as well as I do, Lavinia, Miss Whittle only came here AFTER her uncle had died. Why, she barely knew him!" He was shouting now and, aware he was fuelling the hatred, he turned and hurried away with Verity at his side.

"She is overcome with grief and does not know what she says. I only came as she asked me, just to pay my last respects," Verity was sobbing now, with fright and shame.

At the graveyard scene, a tall bystander came forward and said to the bereaved woman,
"Are you saying there is witchcraft at Old Whittle's place?"
Lavinia recovered her temper with difficulty and glared at the disappearing couple.
"I reckon it could be worse than that," she spat. Turning to the assembled crowd she shouted,
"Know that woman, friends! Know her and shun her company. Do not speak to her and, in truth, run her out of our village. She is the Devil's spawn."

There was a shocked silence. The tall bystander tried to save the situation.
"Peace, Lavinia," he said quietly and several others nodded in agreement. "We came here today to pay our last respects to your daughter, not to fight with a stranger."

Mrs Malkin returned to the group. She knelt down by the grave and murmured,
"Goodbye, Rose. May you bloom forever in the eternal kingdom." The tall man helped her up and the little crowd, as one body, left the lonely graveside.

Verity was home. Lawrence, she knew, was very angry and intended going to the funeral tea to vent his fury.
"Never, in my sixty-two years on this earth, have I seen such a...a...fracas at a funeral!" he cried, struggling for words, "Things will be said, Verity, be assured of that but I would rather do it when I know you are safe from attack."

Verity was close to tears. In her young life, she had only been to three funerals, and none of them had filled her with such horror. Sadness, yes - desolation, yes, but this had shocked her to the core. She found herself unable to speak on the journey home and she walked mechanically, not feeling the wind or cold rain as it fell.

Lawrence took her into the parlour and was glad to see a welcoming blaze burning.
"Sit down and I will get you some tea," he said gently, watching the woman obey as though she was in a trance.

He found Liddy in the kitchen.

"Some tea and make it strong," he ordered, "Does your mistress drink? If so some brandy, please..."

"We don't have any in the house, sir, that we don't. Mistress does not hold with strong liquor but I suppose I could fetch some."

"No don't, please, Liddy, I would rather you stayed with her and called the doctor if she gets any worse."

"The doctor?" cried Liddy, in horror, "Whatever happened today, sir?"

Lawrence enlightened her.

"I think she is in shock, Liddy, I do. Keep her warm and quiet, and get her to eat something, as I am sure she missed breakfast today."

"She did, sir. I set it out fancy-like on a tray but not a morsel was touched nor a drop. She seemed tolerable, and let me put her hair up and get her ready. I knew her heart was elsewhere. That interview with Mrs Malkin shook her, sir."

"Interview, Liddy? From what Frederick said it was more like an attack and, again today, eyes were all over her in disapproval from when she entered the church. How can she be to blame for what her uncle did?"

"She cannot, sir, but happen, here, they believe that the apple doesn't fall far from the tree. She is a stranger too and the villagers do not hold with that."

"Well, I was brought up here, Liddy, and I have never seen such hatred, as was present today. At a funeral too! I am off there now to try and pour oil on troubled waters but I fear I will not be welcome either, because of whose company I keep!"

"I will do what I can, sir, but you know how headstrong my mistress is."

"Stay by her side for the rest of the day, Liddy, and let her talk if she wishes to."

He left, rather reluctantly, calling goodbye to Verity in the parlour but receiving no answer. He hoped the woman had drifted into refreshing slumber but, when Liddy went in some ten minutes later with a heaped up tray, she saw why Lawrence had received no answer. Verity was gone.

CHAPTER EIGHT

Verity had no idea where she was going. All she knew was that the house was claustrophobic and she had to get out. She had no cloak on and only thin shoes but, as her feet walked, her mind finally stopped its ceaseless whirr and calmed down. She began to be aware of the cold and, presently, her own surroundings. She stood on a moorland ridge, looking over a barren landscape, where only a few sheep grazed and some restless birds flew hither and thither, searching for food. Their short, shrill cries hit her with a poignant sadness and she felt tears, warm and salty, on her cheeks.
What had her uncle done to bring this kind of shame on her head? she pondered. The village may have come to accept him as a recluse but, it was clear that, under this title, he meddled in far darker things.

She found a sheltered rock and sat upon it but the cold and damp forced her on her way. Which path now to home? Could she even call it home? She studied the land but it was all unfamiliar to her, and she concluded she must have walked for some time before realisation hit her. Her hair and dress were quite wet. She had not noticed this before, so deep were her preoccupations, but now, these discomforts made her think of warm fires and dry clothes. She shivered. Eventually, the cruel wind made her move and she struck out on the widest of the tracks visible from her vantage point, praying silently that it would lead to the village.

Liddy was in a panic. She had almost dropped the tray when the parlour was empty and she had searched the house and garden, calling her mistress a dozen times. No response. She sat down by the fire and tried to think what to do. Mr Lawrence would be at the funeral tea and, after the volatile anger at the graveside, she had no desire to go to Mrs Malkin's house. That left....
"Mr Frederick!" she cried out loud. She fetched a cloak and some gloves, put on her bonnet and outside shoes and, after securely locking the place up, she left for the village.

"Perhaps I shall see the mistress, taking a walk to calm her mind," she murmured to herself, but no figure came into view and she reached Mr Frederick's lodgings without meeting anyone.

He was not there. His landlady said she was welcome to come in and wait, having known Liddy since she was a child. This she elected to do, as the cold wind had taken her breath away.

"Do you know where he has gone?" she asked. Mrs Binns could not say but she did not think he would be long. With that Liddy had to be content.

The main track that Verity had taken suddenly petered out to a sheep path and she found herself walking...nay, wading, through vegetation and dark, dank puddles of bog water. She picked up her wet dress and tried to carry on but her thin shoes were soaked within seconds, and reluctantly, she turned back and retraced her steps. Maybe she had missed a turning? As far as she could tell, the narrow path off the main track was swinging away from the village, not heading to it.

"Unless it is doing it by means of a roundabout way," she murmured to herself, "Maybe it goes to a lonely farm first and then swings back to the village," She was not confident of her judgement and, worse still, the first signs of dusk were apparent in the cloudy sky.

She turned off the main track, when she had reversed her steps, as there did not seem to be any other option, and she came upon the same problem after a few yards; large wet areas of bog water and, in trying to step on the drier bits in between, she slipped and hurt her side. Seriously handicapped now by the pain, she felt close to tears. Which way should she go? She returned to the rocky outcrops of the plateau and, screwing up her eyes, she searched this way and that for a larger, more definite path. North, west, east, south she turned but nothing much was visible. Then, she spotted a horse and rider, trotting along what must be a bridleway, some yards below her.

Waving her hands to them and shouting, "Wait!" she dashed off, trying not to notice the pain in her side. The rider reined the horse in and turned towards her.

Verity approached the rider with some trepidation but fear of the coming night made her brave.

"I am lost on the moors," she said, by way of explanation, "I have come too far, it seems, and now, cannot find my way back to the village."

"Ah. These bogs can be treacherous if you don't know the lie of the land," replied the stranger.

Verity was puzzled, as he was no villager she was sure but had an accent that spoke of foreign climes. However, this was no time to worry about that.

"Can you furnish me with directions to the place I seek?" she asked, as the horse made to move off again.

"So, where would that be?" asked the rider. He wore a hat pulled low over his face so she could not see much, but she suspected he had a pock-marked face and his eyes were steely blue.

"Coombe Heights," she said simply, and thought that the mention of the name produced an unusual reaction in the man. He jumped and the horse jumped also.

"Ah," said he, recovering quickly, "So, you are Miss Whittle are you? The elusive stranger, rarely seen in the village but the subject of much discussion in the public house!"

Verity felt vaguely annoyed.

"I take no part in gossip..." she began.

"No, madam, but you certainly gave it food for thought by taking your uncle's old place, all on your own."

"I have a maid there living-in. She will be out searching for me now, as I speak." Somehow, Verity felt threatened by this man but why she could not say.

"Take this bridle path in the other direction to which I am travelling and you will arrive at the crossroads. Then, take the first track on the right and that will take you round the swell, thus, more or less to the door of the dwelling you seek," he replied. The way he pronounced 'dwelling' made

Verity stare, as he said it with vicious intent, and she was very puzzled.

"Thank you for your help Mr...?" she replied.

"Darling...Alphonso Darling," he almost shouted at her, and then he released the rein, kicked his horse into a gallop, and disappeared.

Confused and in some pain, Verity turned and took the route he suggested.

Liddy stared at the darkening sky out of the small, rather dirty window in Frederick's room and her heart sank. Where was the man and why had Mrs Binns told her he would not be long? She sighed, got up from the chair she had been waiting in and made for the door. As she did, she heard a door open downstairs and the sound of Frederick's deep voice, calling to his landlady. Relief washed over her like a river and she called out to the man.

She heard him ascend and cast surprised eyes over her as she stood, framed, in the doorway.

"Liddy! Why, what is amiss? Is it Verity? Did you call the doctor as Lawrence suggested?"

"You have seen your friend then and know what occurred?"

"Yes, I saw him coming back from the funeral tea and we made plans..."

"Oh, Mr Frederick," burst in Liddy, "It is my mistress – that is, she is missing!"

"What?"

"I went in with a hearty meal as Mr Lawrence suggested, and she wasn't there!"

"What do you mean?"

"She had left the parlour and..."

"You searched the rest of the house before coming here?" He had reached her by now and she could see the anxiety in his face.

"Yes, sir. I searched everywhere before I came to you but that was hours ago."

"You have been waiting a long time for my return?"

"Yes, as Mrs Binns said you would not be long."

"And neither would I have been, had I not run into Lawrence."

"So, she has been gone for hours, sir, and I am very worried."

"There is no one at Coombe Heights, if she returns?"

"No, sir, and I am afraid I locked the doors too."

Frederick nodded.

"Our first thing then is to go back and see if she has returned. It is getting dark, Liddy, and not safe for anyone to be abroad."

He brushed past her into his room and, taking some items from a drawer, put them in a knapsack and, then, with a wary eye to the sky, the two left for Verity's house.

The place was empty when they reached it and Liddy bewailed the time it had taken to get there, time that should have been spent trying to find her mistress.

"I don't believe she knows how to get back here, sir. I feel she is lost."

"Nevertheless, Liddy, I want you to remain here, in case she does come back, and I will go and search."

"But, sir, it will be better with two of us."

"No, Liddy, please do not be as stubborn as your mistress! Remain here, as Lawrence talked of calling to see how Miss Whittle is, and you can tell him what happened and he can then search too."

"But where will you look, sir, if he asks?"

It was dark now, with a fragile dusk that came down at 4 o'clock in January and obscured the landscape.

"I...I don't know," replied Frederick, "Tell him I will take the paths on the northern side of the village, and he can go southward when he comes."

"But I could do that, sir, now."

"No, Liddy. Your devotion to your mistress does you credit but we want no heroics here. Have you forgotten what stirs in the dark out there, every night?"

"No, sir, and it is because of that that I wish to go. Mistress will be terrified. Yes, I am, that I'll own, but she will be too and with me, we can cover twice as much ground."

However, Frederick would not have it, and Liddy was forced to concede and remain in the hope Verity found her way home.

It was pitch dark when Frederick set out and his naturally cheerful disposition was somewhat blunted by the day's turn of events. He considered Mrs Malkin was to blame for Verity's plight and he wished that he had been at the funeral but he was aware the tongues of Scar's End were wagging far too frequently for his liking. With any luck, he would despatch the rest of the vampires and then be on his way.

He stopped many a time, thinking he heard the rustle of Verity's skirts but it was sheep grazing in the dark or wandering from one area to the other. He knew roughly where the bogs were but did Verity? He thought not and that worried him. He prayed Lawrence would join him in the search soon or that he would return in a few hours and Liddy would say to him,
"Mistress is in bed and asleep."

There was very little moon that night, with the sky being overcast and numerous rain clouds moving in the firmament; he could feel the wind getting up. After about twenty minutes he arrived at the crossroads and thought he saw a figure standing there but it was his over-worked imagination playing tricks with him. What a lonely spot it was on a dark winter's night! To think that Verity wanted to accompany him and Lawrence here! For the first time he thought about life without Verity and, he was ashamed to say, it did not appeal to him. How she felt he did not know but their minds, at least, were compatible.

The whirr of wind, moving the crossroad sign, disturbed his reverie and he called into the eldritch darkness,
"Verity! Verity! Verity!" but his words were flung away from him and a slight echo mocked him with its answer,

"Verity! Verity! Verity!" Which way had she gone, and where was the path to reach her? He turned all ways, felt a sudden connection with the eastwards path and struck it, swinging his lantern and calling. Only sheep ran from his path and once, he heard the mysterious cry of a goatsucker, with several of the birds whirring close to his face. It only served to hasten his steps as he knew if Verity heard them, she would remember the bats and be terrified.

Suddenly, his foot struck something warm and soft and he almost fell over. Righting himself, with difficulty, he opened the slats on his lantern and shone the light, then recoiled with horror. It was another sheep but this one was dead, and its throat had been bitten in several places. The corpse was obviously drained of blood. Frederick found his teeth chattering and, leaving this grisly find, he ran off into the night, his calls echoing with a new desperation.

Verity was indeed scared, out in the suffocating darkness. Part of her wanted to curl up into a ball and see the long night out, safe behind a rock or in a cave – should she be lucky enough to find one, of course. But, as it got later and later, fear took over and she was terrified of what would emerge out of the darkness, so pushed on.
Would anyone be looking for her, she wondered? Seeing as she had left no note, nor told anyone where she was going, she realised that was unlikely. Even if they did come to search, she had meandered around so much in the darkness, that she did not even know herself where she was. The directions of the foreign gentleman had long since disappeared from her mind but his steely blue eyes had not.

She heard a sharp noise to her left and fear asserted itself again. It was only a sheep crossing her path but her heart raced and she felt sick. The mournful cry of birds assailed her ears and the ground was becoming increasingly marshy. She skirted what she could, but her stockings and shoes were soaked, and the end of her dress was heavy with filthy water.

Seeing some rocks on her left, she decided to rest a while and recover some strength, hoping to get her bearings once more. She stared up at the stars and remembered the Plough but what direction it pointed had slipped her racing mind. Besides, the sky was very cloudy and the stars shone but dimly, certainly not brightly enough to make out any constellation.

She sank down on the dry ground behind the boulders and tried to calm down. A strange fluttering, as of sharp bony wings, interrupted her thoughts and, peering out from behind the rocks, she could just make out two outlines in the darkness, standing but a few feet from her. She ducked back and covered her mouth as their conversation hit her.

"They've killed Rose and buried her in hallowed ground," came a woman's voice, "Taken her away from her eternal life and tried to force their God on her."

"Love killed her, way before the stake went in," replied a man, "We should have been the ones doing the killings, not these hunters. Now, it is just you and me and the Master, when he comes, to wander for eternity."

"Have you feasted recently?" asked the woman, who sounded young.

"Only a sheep tonight, on the moor's edge, but rich pickings a few nights ago. A child from a gypsy camp, left to wander alone at Bollard's Hill."

"Ah...so he will join us."

"Yes, I drained him like a vat of beer and left him hidden in bracken; no doubt the crows will find him and they are welcome to my leftovers!"

"A young 'un, eh?"

"Nought but six, and I took a few bites from his brother but he got away."

"Not for long when the bloodlust comes over him."

"No. More and more will join the ranks – the Master will see to that."

Verity almost gasped aloud with horror. Two children! "His blood kept me satisfied for a couple of days but I crave again. A sheep does not satisfy like a human!"

'Oh my God,' thought Verity, 'They will smell my blood.' She curled into a tiny ball and hid her face.

101

"The village has shut its windows and no-one walks abroad at night anymore," continued the woman, "We can smell the blood of the humans but we cannot get to it. Instead they lured us with pig's blood! A poor substitute but we were hungry and not eaten for days. Rose was famished, and it cost her her life!"

"To think it was done on what used to be my property," bewailed the man.

Verity sat up at this. Could this be her uncle speaking?

"They keep me away with 'love' - filthy love." He fair spat the word out, "Every night the odious substance descends to burn and maim me. A pink mist it is, and I can hardly breathe or eat. I am wasting away!"

The woman laughed.

"No-one loves me," she said, almost in triumph, "No mist blinds my eyes or closes my throat but I have been on the walls of your house, as was, and seen the bitch who has taken over your place."

"Ah, I bequeathed it to her before the shadow of the Master came upon me, when I was in my human body. Bah, I was glad enough to leave that behind and transcend but I am hungry, despite the sheep, and I smell something," Verity shook at those words. "I think it must be far off and we must take to the skies, if we are to locate it."

The woman agreed.

"Yes, I smell a trace of human blood, too," she told her companion, "Come, let us take to the air and find it!"

Verity heard the snap of bony wings, and she knew they had returned to their altered state but she dare not look, for fear they were still there. She screwed herself up into an even tinier ball and counted to a hundred, very slowly, and waited. She listened again but only the mournful wail of the wind reached her ears. Cautiously, she peered out but nothing was visible. If she moved would they still find her, since they were perusing the moors for warm, living, fresh blood? She felt sick with the thought of it. What if Liddy were out looking for her? Verity prayed that her maid had run for either Frederick or Lawrence, as both of them would be equal to the dubious charms of a vampire.

She was stiff from sitting on the hard ground and resolved, come what may, she must leave the shelter of the rocks and seek another path.
"Love, love, love," she cried to herself, sending the very pink light that had kept her uncle away from her since he appeared in her dreams. Dreams, she thought - no nightmares - yet to think, he had only been feet away from her! She stopped for a moment, gathered her thoughts, then put a silver and blue cloak of protection around herself and prayed to Michael, the great archangel, to keep her safe and help her find the road to home. Feeling somewhat calmed, she struck out on a promising path.

Frederick suspected the vampires were on the moorland, even before he found the dead sheep. There were no pickings for them in the village itself and he had heard the rumour that a gypsy boy had been bitten by a nocturnal creature, under cover of darkness, a few nights ago, over at Bollard's Hill. That he intended to check out tomorrow, or today, judging by the way the night was progressing. Feeling wary, he took out his cross and the phial of Holy Water to protect himself should the skies suddenly rain down vampires. How many were there in this area? No one knew. Where, oh where, was Verity? In his mind he saw her bitten and bleeding but he dismissed the picture quickly, as it was too negative and, he knew, would only attract more depressing thoughts. Birds of a feather, and all that.

He began to call again, trying to keep the desperation out of his voice. Using the power of his mind, he began willing her to come to him. He had trained himself to do this over the years of vampire hunting and he knew it worked. 'Get away from the danger,' he told Verity, 'Walk my way,' He could see and feel the blue and silver cloak she had clad herself in, and Michael stood with his sword at her left shoulder.

103

Out in the darkness, Verity's frantic footsteps suddenly faltered and stopped. She was going the wrong way! Did she think it or say it out loud? She did not know but it seemed gentle yet strong hands turned her around and, now, her eyes alighted on a small but definite path to the left, that she had not seen before. It left the main track and descended to another track she could just see in the distance, when the sliver of moon shone through the clouds. Here was shelter, here was safety, peace soothed her mind. Even though she had no reason to believe anyone was about, she began to call out, "Liddy! Frederick! Lawrence! I am here! I am here!" as though to proclaim her presence to the world and, suddenly, she was not frightened anymore.

Frederick stopped. Had his over-zealous imagination raised a voice in the darkness? No, there it was again – faint but audible. He began to run, holding out his cross in front of him and yelling,
"Verity! Verity! Where are you?"
A whispered response came back to him and he stopped to work out the direction of the voice. To the left! And coming closer!
He called again, his voice sharp with anticipation. If it was Verity, at least she was alive. And back came the answer he needed to dispel the dark thoughts that threatened to engulf him.
"Frederick – is that you? I am here! Coming down the path to your left!"

Two minutes later they had met up. Frederick hugged her to his heart, as though he never wanted to let her go. For two full minutes he gripped her, so tightly that she could not breathe.
"Frederick!" a muffled yell and a gasp and he loosened his hold.
"You are not hurt?"
"No."
"Nor bitten?"

104

"No, but I have seen two vampires, one of which could have been my uncle, and I hid and prayed!"

No sooner had she said these words than it seemed the air was alive with them, claws and teeth shining in the errant moonlight. Verity screamed and Frederick let her go and thrust the cross skyward crying,
"In the name of love, GO! I send you the pink mist of LOVE, the deep LOVE vibration to permeate every fibre of your black soul!"

The nearest bat began to writhe in agony, then twist and turn in the air. It had no choice but to leave or fall from the sky and be prey to the vampire hunter. It was suffocated and choking and the two flew off, away from the very essence of purity.

Frederick grabbed Verity's hand.
"We are safe now," he cried, "However, they will return. Hurry, we must go. I know the way back. Here, take the lantern, and open the shutters, so you can illuminate our path. I will follow on behind you, with the cross." He took her hand and she swung the lantern to dispel the darkness of midnight and together, exhausted, wet and cold they made their way back to the village.

"There's no real cause for concern," The doctor snapped his bag shut and faced the two tired people who were waiting in the parlour, "The night air, lingering shock, lack of food and over-exertion, have all combined to make her ill. Why was she wandering on the moors at that time of night, anyway?"

Liddy looked at Frederick, who shrugged his shoulders.
"We don't know," he said simply.
"She had been to a funeral, as we told you," volunteered Liddy.
"But no-one close," cut in Frederick.

The doctor looked from one to the other. He had heard something of the rumpus at the funeral when he was called to Mrs Malkin's little daughter last night, who was coughing badly.

"If Miss Whittle gets any worse, I will call back tomorrow," he said, "But, for today, I think it better that she sleeps." It was obvious no more information was going to come forth and he was a busy man.

Liddy showed him out, then returned to the parlour. It was past noon the next day and Verity had tossed and turned for the rest of the night, in a fevered delirium. Frederick had slept for a few hours on the settle and was now anxious to get away to investigate the rumour of the gypsy child. "Can I leave you now, Liddy?" he asked, "I will be back later to see how Verity is and talk to her then."

The maid frowned.

"Yes, sir," she said obediently, "She sleeps at present."

Frederick showed himself out and left Liddy to her thoughts. Walking to the village, he went straight to see Lawrence and filled him in on the night's activities. Frederick had stopped briefly at his lodgings at dawn, to assure his landlady he was still alive, and had secured a bit more information about the gypsy boy. He knew travellers were a closed door when it came to talking to the outside world and he was grateful for a helping hand from Mrs Binns.

He informed his friend what he had uncovered.

"My landlady gives odd jobs to one of the young gypsy boys. I think he is about thirteen and his father happened to mention it, when he came to pick the boy up. 'Eh, lady, we are in trouble up on Bollard's Hill,' he told her. It seems one boy is missing and another, his brother, is troubled by night terrors, so they have to tie him down during the hours of darkness," Frederick imparted.

"The boy told his father that a creature with red eyes came down from the skies and took Richard – that's his brother – but he managed to escape, although the thing went after him and bit him on the neck."

"That's not good," replied Lawrence. "Not good at all. We must get over there or the situation could spiral out of control."

Within an hour they had departed for Bollard's Hill and, although Frederick was anxious concerning what they faced here, his mind frequently turned to Verity. Would she recover from her terrifying episode? It meant nothing to him, it was the sort of occurrence he dealt with most days, but to a highly strung woman, as he considered Verity was, it could haunt her for life.

The ride out to Bollard's Hill was uneventful and both men seemed preoccupied and conversed little. Lawrence was ruminating over the scene at the graveside and wondering if he should have done more to curtail it. Would Miss Whittle then have stayed safe and secure in her bed, instead of wandering in a distressed state? Frederick was acutely aware that he needed to talk to Verity about the vampires she had seen but her collapse, as soon as they arrived home, had stopped him. Liddy had then taken charge, insisted he run for the doctor and had forbidden him to see her mistress.

The carriage dropped them off outside the gypsy camp, promising to return an hour later to pick them up. Frederick hoped that his connection with the kindly Mrs Binns would facilitate introductions here with the Enderby clan.

They found an elderly woman hanging out ragged washing on some bushes, followed by a group of bawling children and, after a lengthy conversation - mostly shouted as the old woman was deaf - she deemed to fetch her son.

He turned out to be the father of the two boys and, when help was offered, he seized Frederick's hand and said they were at their wits' end to know what to do.
"So, the younger boy has not been seen since?" asked Frederick.
"No, sir. We walked the paths in Lea Woods, where the attack happened, but no sign. My wife is beside herself and the other boy will not rest. I have to tie him to the bed at night with our belts. What is it? Do you know?"

Frederick looked at Lawrence but both remained grim-faced.
"If we could just see your son, please."

"Of course. He is relatively calm during the day but nightfall brings a strange change over him."

The boy, when brought forward, seemed in control of himself but shook his head when asked how he felt when sleeping. He was seized by nightmares, he said, but knew nothing else. He answered the other questions about what happened and told them that Richard and he had been playing in Lea Woods, during the early evening, although their parents thought they were in bed. Suddenly, a creature, like a man but with red eyes, came from the trees and chased them.

"We were getting away, sir, when Richard fell, as he had the pox last week and was weak, and I could not leave him, so I ran back but the creature had hold of him and his hands were like claws...all long and gnarled. He then left my brother and came after me, getting hold of me but, as I am bigger and stronger than Richard, I managed to fight him off. As I was making my escape the thing then sprouted wings and appeared in front of me. He bit my neck, sir, and it hurt very much but still I fought him off. He had long, white teeth, like a picture of a wolf in my granddad's picture book, and his eyes were as red as the sunset. His breath smelt of decay, and I felt him coming in for a second bite when he became aware of my gold cross, which fell across his bony hand. He screamed then, at the touch of it, like he had been burnt; he let me go and I ran for it. When I returned a few minutes later, both him and my brother were gone."

"So, Richard does not wear a cross then?"

"No, sir," answered the father, "There is only one in our family and it is handed down to the eldest son, my first born, at eight years of age. It is an old gypsy tradition, sir."

Lawrence raised his eyebrows.

"Can we see your neck, Joshua, please?" he asked.

The boy obediently undid the neckerchief tied around his throat and both the men peered closer. Two deep penetration holes showed in the bluey skin and they had yet to heal. They were undeniably the marks of a vampire's teeth.

108

It was two hours later and Frederick was heading back to see Verity. He had left Lawrence with the boy and his parents and had mounted the coach back to Scar's End. Later, he would return to the gypsy camp to take a turn in watching the lad overnight to judge what ailed him. At least, that was what he had told the parents but, in truth, he knew exactly what had taken over the boy. It was what he and Lawrence were going to do about it that worried Frederick.

He stood outside Verity's front door and heard Liddy's hurried step approaching.

"Ah, Mr Frederick," She seemed flustered, "Mistress was just asking about you."

"How is she?"

"Tolerable, sir. She insisted on getting up and now sits by the fire in the parlour. She seems troubled in her mind and is anxious to speak with you."

Frederick handed over his hat and coat. He was already exhausted and there was a long night ahead of him.

"Tea, sir?" asked Liddy, as she opened the parlour door.

"Yes, please. I would be glad of some refreshment."

Liddy hurried away and the warmth of the room embraced Frederick but it made him feel even more drowsy. Verity was sitting on the settle with her feet up, fully dressed with a shawl around her shoulders.

"My dear lady," began Frederick, capturing her hand and kissing it, "Have you recovered from last night?"

Verity looked tired but bright enough.

"Yes, thank you, Frederick, but I had to see you urgently and Liddy said you had waited whilst I slept and had then gone on your way."

"She would not let me see you after the doctor called," the man replied and then, as Verity's face grew dark with anger, he smiled and continued, "Don't berate your maid as she has a loyalty that is touching to behold."

Verity managed a laugh at this and her eyes lit up.

"But I wouldn't put it past her to be listening at the door now!" she told him. In answer Frederick got up, opened the great barrier, looked out and affirmed the hallway was empty.

"So, you can say what you like to me," he told Verity, returning to his seat.

"It is the two boys," began Verity, "I could hardly sleep – exhausted as I was – for thinking about them. One bitten and one dead."

"We don't know that. No body has been found."

"But the vampire who was once my uncle said he drained him and left him as raven fodder, or was it for the crows? I can't quite remember."

"I have been up there, Verity, with Lawrence. To Bollard's Hill, I mean. In fact, I have left Lawrence there now and I will join him later. The boy who was bitten is showing signs of vampirism."

Verity's dark eyes were full of compassion.

"Can you save him?" she asked, in a tearful whisper.

Frederick looked less than hopeful.

"I don't know," he said, with honesty.

At this point Liddy came in with the tea tray and all talk was suspended for a few minutes. Frederick poured but Verity struggled to swallow a mouthful, so full was her heart, and her cake crumbled upon her plate and staled.

"So, what about the other boy?" she asked, when they had heard Liddy go back into the kitchen.

"Lea Woods has been searched, it seems, by the gypsies and nothing was found."

"Don't tell me the vampire, that is - my uncle, took the boy?"

"Do you remember his exact words, Verity?"

She shook her head.

"Yet, wait a minute," she carried on, "He said something about leaving him in the bracken." She put her full cup down.

"I will be honest; this has shaken me to the core, Frederick. To think my uncle is now one of the great Undead and that he flies through the world, feasting off the bodies of innocent children."

"He will take what he can, Verity. He is not your uncle. He was once but now another force controls him – a force stronger than death itself."

"He said he killed a sheep too."

"I know, as I found it."

"Oh, Frederick, how terrible for you. I should have gone mad if I had seen that."

"I was very anxious that you didn't. We went back another way."

There was an uneasy silence in the room. Verity was struggling not to cry and Frederick was trying to think what else he needed to ask her.

"Did you actually see the vampires, Verity?"

"No, as I ducked down behind some rocks and listened to their conversation. They were not there long."

"Did you see anyone else on the moors that night?"

"No," Verity was unsure of her answer. Her brain was befuddled with lack of sleep but vague memories were coming back to her.

"Wait," she cried, spilling her tea, "Yes, I did! I did see someone else. Of course I did! The man with the steely blue eyes!" She sat up and shivered.

"His eyes," she whispered, "I could not forget his eyes."

"So, who was he?" Frederick asked gently. "Did you get a name?"

Verity frowned.

"Not one I can remember," she told him, "He was a foreign gentleman, that I do recall...and I asked him if he could direct me to the village."

"And did he?"

"Well, he furnished some sort of directions but I struggled to follow them..."

"Anything else, Verity? Do you remember anything else about him?"

Verity shook her head.

"I think he wore a hat," she faltered, "Or did he have a muffler on? I didn't clearly see his face, just his eyes."

"Was he walking?"

"No, he rode a horse."

There was silence. Verity was screwing her face up, trying to remember. Nothing else came to her.

"Think carefully, Verity. This could be very very important," Frederick was leaning forward in his seat.

"I can't, Frederick. It hurts to think and I can't remember any more. Why do you think this is so vital?"

Frederick sat back.

"I don't know," he said, "I am not sure but he could be connected. Out on the moor at night?"

"I don't think it was completely dark when I met him. Not the dead of night, as it were, anyway. But the vampires I listened to later talked of a Master. Do you think this man could be..."

"The Master? Possibly, but without his name or a location I cannot check him out. Do think again, Verity."

Verity tried to concentrate.

"It is there. I can get fragments of it. A strange name, I remember, but it eludes me at present. I was so worried over the boys that everything else about the night just seemed to wash over me."

Frederick could see she was becoming anxious and tried to soothe her.

"Don't worry, Verity. Maybe just let it float to the surface of your mind and then send Liddy over with the name."

"You have to go now?"

"I must get back to Bollard's Hill."

"You think there is trouble there?"

"Yes, sadly. I must search for the missing boy in the bracken in Lea's Wood."

"His poor parents," Verity's kind heart was overcome with sorrow.

Frederick kissed her hand again. She felt icily cold and he was worried about the shock lingering.

"I will return when I have some news," he promised, "However, as things are, I cannot promise it will be good."

"My uncle, murdering children," murmured Verity to herself but Frederick told her to trouble her head no more about it. "Just keep him away from you, Verity, by using the love vibration. Don't forget."

Verity shook her head.

"I won't," she affirmed.

"Goodbye," he called from the parlour door but she did not reply and seemed lost in thought. Frederick hesitated for a moment, then quit the house with a troubled heart.

The journey back to Bollard's Hill was a dismal one. For one thing, it was raining in large, freezing drops and for another, Frederick was worried about finding a body after his conversation with Verity. Draining the young boy of blood and dumping him in the bracken for crows to peck at! He shuddered. Yet he had faced worse than this before and got through it. But there was no pretty girl involved then, his mind told him honestly. He resolved to search the woods first, in case the worried parents had not done a thorough job.

When he arrived at the camp, he could see by Lawrence's face that there was no need to look. Wailing greeted his ears, he knew that the boy had been found and the news was not good. It looked like Verity's prophecy had been proved right.

The body was laid out on a pallet, strewn with flowers and leaves. The pallor of the skin, almost blue when the late January sun hit it, convinced Frederick that the boy had, indeed, been drained of blood. The two telltale marks were there in the neck too.

Frederick pulled Lawrence away for a quiet word. "What do we do?" he whispered, "You know the only way to deal with this, and the parents are not going to want the body mutilated. Have you told them anything?"

"Such as? Sorry, your son was killed by a vampire and has become one of the great Undead. Oh, yes, and your other son will shortly be following suit."

"They haven't noticed the puncture wounds?"

"No, or if they have, they have attributed them to some wild animal's bite."

"And have you found out how long this wake will go on for?"

"Three days from what I can gather."

"Long enough for the boy to rise and do his worst here."

"We have to speak to the father at least," Frederick decided, "We have to make him aware of the danger the whole camp is in. We have to ask him to keep this secret too."

"I presume you have never dealt with gypsies before in your travels," Lawrence asked, "At least they seem to keep themselves to themselves. Who knew they were even here? They do not go to the village and no-one from the village would ever come here. For Scar's End's views on gypsies are they are filthy ragamuffins."

"Yes, but if the village finds out there are vampires here, the gypsies will be blamed for it, and then the people will come in hordes and force these travellers out or even attack them."

"Hopefully we will have dealt with the situation by then," Frederick replied, "Shall I see the father and you stay with the boy? Then, when darkness falls, we must prepare for the worst if the parents will not allow us to stake the boy."

When Frederick approached the man to try and convince him what sort of creature had attacked both his sons, he was met by a wall of silence and disbelief. The father refused the notion of anything other than a wild animal killing his son and injuring the other. Frederick showed him the teeth marks on both boys but the gypsy shook his head.

"What you say is a fabrication - a lie!" he cried, putting his hands over his ears, as if to keep out the words, "And now you want to dismember my son and dishonour his memory, thus ruining his hopes of eternal life! We are God-fearing people and to do what you say makes a mockery of every creed I was brought up in. No, you are wrong. A wild beast killed my boy and wounded the other, who will recover without any help from you. I thought you came here as doctors of the mind and body to help us but I see I was wrong! You are vile interlopers sent to spy on us, and to spread tales in order to get us out! Now I want you out!"

The scene was beginning to turn ugly and a couple of the other men raised cudgels against them, so there was no option but to leave.

Walking back, Lawrence surmised what would happen to the two boys now but Frederick shook his head and said he was not prepared to give up that easily.

"In three days they will inter him. We must find out where and perform our ritual that ensures he lays peacefully in the grave. They will not guard the tomb night and day."

"By night he will fly and feast."

"I propose we come out later tonight and watch. They will dig some final resting place for the boy, no doubt, and we may hear some stray snatch of conversation."

"What of the other boy?"

Frederick shrugged his shoulders.

"All we can do is send him love and pray he has no more attacks."

"You mean his brother could come back for him?"

"Exactly. Death will not break that bond but now it will be twisted and one brother could feed on the other."

"How will the parents deal with that? Do you think they will spread the word?"

"No. He desires this afternoon's conversation to stay between the two of us. The only word he has spread is that we are prejudiced against his race of people. That is why they raised the cudgels against us. They have this attitude to cope with wherever they move, so why should this place be any different?"

"But what if they pull up roots and leave?" asked Lawrence, "Did you find out their plan when you talked to the father?"

"They are working on a farm near the woods and stripping the fields of cabbages and the like. The man told me there is

115

another two week's work for them all and then they will head south."

"Leaving their boy cold in the sod then?"

"They believe after the wake the boy will attain eternal life in glory. So why would they worry about a shell? We have only two weeks to sort this out, Lawrence, and I just don't know if it can be done."

By now the dark was descending and they had reached the outskirts of the village. They parted at the church and, whilst Lawrence took the path to his home, Frederick returned to see how Verity was faring and impart the sad news about the boy.

Both Lawrence and Frederick went to see Verity in the end. For one thing Lawrence was very despondent over the turn of events and did not relish his own company, even for a few hours. Thus, he turned back at the door of his house and went after his friend. Frederick, having been in the vampire business far longer than his companion, knew there were going to be cases he could not win.

"Lives sometimes have to be sacrificed," he told Lawrence but he had not given up and the plan was to return under cover of darkness and see what had occurred. An hour or so with Verity and then a meal at his lodgings would fill the time nicely, Frederick felt.

"It is very different for you," Lawrence was saying now, as they made their way to Coombe Heights, "In a few days or maybe a week, you will leave here and, in moving on, you will forget us but I was raised here, in this black slice of heath, and I love it and the people here. I seek to protect it from the evil that is threatening us all. At the moment my mind is undecided as to whether I come with you on the next assignment or not."

Frederick understood but he would not consider failure, as he felt it had not come their way as yet.

"We are simply opting for different tactics," he told his friend, as they walked up Verity's path.

"They have closed the front door in our faces, it is true, but we can yet get round the back, so all hope is not extinguished, dear friend."

Liddy came to answer the door, dusting flour off her hands as she did so.

"Ah, you have been baking again?" questioned Frederick.

"Yes, sir," replied Liddy. "Another batch of cakes just put in. I am sure you smelt them! Come in. Mistress was asleep when I went in earlier but she's awake now."

"Has she eaten?"

"Hardly a mouthful, sir."

Frederick frowned. Things were bad enough without having Verity ill too. The men entered the parlour and Verity struggled up, wiping the sleep out of her eyes.

"What news?" she asked, as the men sat by the fire and warmed their cold hands.

"They have shown us the door," said Lawrence, in a sad voice.

"Or, in their case, the gate," replied Frederick, making a grim attempt at humour.

Verity bit her lip.

"So, what will you do now?" she asked.

"I did warn you that it may be bad news, Verity," Frederick carried on, "I wanted to prepare you if things did turn sour on us. The body of the boy was found."

"In some undergrowth in Lea Woods," qualified Lawrence, who had been there.

"In some bracken?" from Verity.

"Yes, and the bites of the Devil were upon him," Lawrence continued, "It was the father who found him and the wailing that broke out. I can't tell you how bad it was, my ears are still ringing with it."

"I heard it when the coach stopped," agreed Frederick, "We tried to tell the father exactly what he faced..."

"But he would not believe you," cut in Verity, "And who would Frederick? You are selling them a fairy story, a tale of witches and goblins, that they are never going to buy!"

Frederick nodded. "You are right," he told her, "The father, who appears to be the head of the clan, thought we were making fun of them for being gypsies. He believed that we were saying they were inferior to us and, thus, we saw fit to spin them a tale which we thought they were stupid enough to believe! We had no choice but to leave!"

Liddy brought a heaped up tray in at that point and tried to linger, so that she could hear what was going on but Verity sent her off.

"Frederick can pour, Liddy, thank you, so there is no necessity for you to stay."

Liddy flounced off and they heard the petulant slam of the kitchen door.

"So, what will you do now?" asked Verity, accepting a cup of tea from Frederick with a smile.

"Go back tonight under cover of darkness and see what is happening. The wake is three days long, they told Lawrence and at the end, they must inter the boy's body somewhere."

"What? In Lea Woods? No proper burial? No hallowed ground?"

"It is the gypsy way I was told," replied Lawrence, absent-mindedly eating all the leftover cakes.

Darkness soon came, as dusk does in January, and bright particles of frost graced the freezing air. Verity knew Frederick was going back to the gypsy camp and she worried. What if the men were seen or heard? Her experience of gypsies was sketchy but she did not trust them and perceived the entire race as a strange and alien concept. Many was the time she remembered her mother telling her to behave or she would be 'left for the gypsies'. Her mother never elaborated on what the gypsies would do to her but it was clearly a threat and not judged to be pleasant at all. Often had she heard her mother mention a changeling, a foundling, a gypsy child, in a hushed voice, as though she was afraid. Of course, to the eavesdropper, this was never explained as it was part of adult conversation but the mystery and the dread grew.

When she was a little older, Verity had passed such encampments and fear had rattled up in her throat, so she had hurried past with her head down. She had never run, as then the gypsies would know she was afraid of them and they would come after her. Or so her ten year old mind thought. Now she prayed that the men would be safe tonight and they would come up with a plan to save the boy.

"Will you come back and see me tomorrow, when you have slept?" she asked Frederick, as the men took their leave.

"Yes, certainly, if there is any news," replied Frederick, kissing her hand.

"It may, of course, take a few nights to glean any information," warned Lawrence.

"I am not even sure of how we proceed from here," qualified Frederick, "We could go tonight and find the whole camp has moved on and Lea Woods are quiet and deserted."

"Then what will you do? Go after them?" There was concern in Verity's dark eyes.

Frederick shook his head.

"It is unlikely to happen," he acknowledged, "They have work there for a while and money coming in but once that dries up they will move on. I hope by then, events will have taken a more sanguine turn but we have to be prepared. There may be nothing further we can do."

"I shall strive to remember the man I saw," promised Verity, seeing, as she spoke, his blue eyes and his olive skin; well, what was visible of his face anyway, "His name eludes me, but I am confident it will come back to me."

As it was, the night drew a blank and despite eight hours of watching, hidden deep in the shrubbery surrounding the gypsy camp, very little activity was seen and certainly no opportunity presented itself to get any closer. Lanterns flared up and singing and mournful chanting could be heard most of the night but both Lawrence and Frederick were chilled to the bone by the time 6 o'clock rang out. They were also thoroughly disillusioned by the night's revelations.

"I feel everything hinges on Verity remembering the name of this man who she encountered on the moors, and the fact that

119

he appeared to give her false directions to the village is suspicious in itself," said Frederick as they gained the safety of the village.

"You believe he is critical to our enquiries?" asked Lawrence.

"I certainly think he is worth checking out but, only by having his name, can we go any further. Then we can find out where he lives. Are there any other old crumbling mansions such as Coombe Heights hereabout?" Frederick continued.

"One or two," Lawrence told him, "Falling into disrepair as far as I am aware but possibly part of them could be decent enough to be rented out by the owner."

"Come back to my lodgings and we'll mull it over with a tot of brandy whilst my landlady cooks us some food," Frederick offered.

Half an hour later, they sat by a roaring fire sipping brandy and hot water and waiting for the repast, as Mrs Binns always rose sharp at six. A knock came at the door and Frederick rose to answer it; he saw a flushed but triumphant Liddy, her eyes bright with excitement.

"Mistress has remembered!" she cried, "She knows the name that you need now and begs you to come over at once."

The men looked at each other and drained their brandies, for it was still very cold outside. Could this be the clue they needed?

CHAPTER TEN

Verity greeted them much more like her old self. Her eyes sparkled and she shook them both by the hand warmly. "Alphonso Darling," she said, after she had thanked them both for coming so promptly.

"Darling?" mused Lawrence, "Darling? I seem to recollect a foreign man of that name in my travels. Rides a black horse."

"That's him," agreed Verity, "A very curt, austere gentleman with a thick accent, muffled up in a kerchief...and he wore spurs," she almost shouted, as memories flooded back to her. "So, he gave you no other clues as to where he was living or even what his business was on the moors?"

Verity shook her head.

"He seemed lost in his own world," she continued, "He hardly noticed me, and the directions he gave me were not correct."

Lawrence looked thoughtful.

"I can make some enquiries in the village," he said.

"There is every possibility my landlady may know the gentleman," Frederick commented, "She seems to know everyone and gave me a history of the gypsies who frequent these parts."

Liddy, who had come back with them, now brought in some refreshments and the talk turned to Verity's health.

"Much improved, I thank you," said the lady, "Sleep has helped, although I saw the steely, blue eyes of Alphonso staring at me as I dreamt, but I also heard the words he said to me and thus was able to get his name. I pray he is the lead to the Master."

"He could even be that person," replied Frederick, "And now I propose we return to my lodgings, Lawrence, and begin our enquiries, unless you need to sleep first?"

"By all means," Lawrence agreed, "I could not rest knowing that we held this massive clue in the palms of our hands and had not progressed to try and solve the mystery. Let us go."

They left a few minutes after tea and Liddy, who had been boldly listening at the door, was intrigued by the message she had carried and was now very anxious to know where the Master fitted into the vampire hierarchy. She asked her mistress when she came in to take the tea tray.

Verity seemed vexed.

"It is nothing for you to concern yourself about," she retorted sharply and after this, she closed her lips on the subject. Liddy was vexed too and gave an impatient shake of her head but she realised that, to keep her position she must be contrite.

"Sorry, miss, I am sure," she forced out, and then she changed the subject, asking what Verity required for luncheon.

Mrs Binns was far from pleased when her lodger ran off, leaving his cooked breakfast but she tried to keep the two meals warm and the men returned within the hour, apologising profusely for their sudden departure.

"'Twas that Liddy I suppose, drove you out. She was hopping from one foot to another when I let her in. No doubt her mistress needed you."

The last sentence was uttered with heavy emphasis on the word 'needed' but Frederick chose to let it pass him by. He knew some people in the village were gossiping about him and Verity but the severity of the vampire problem that he faced here was taking all his attention and energy. In another few weeks he would be gone, so why, when he thought of that, did he feel choked and why did tears spring to his eyes?

"Will you not take a cup of tea with us now, Mrs Binns?" he asked, receiving his heaped up plate.

"Very well, sir, if that is agreeable to you."

"We need to ask you a few questions and it might be as well to do it whilst consuming this excellent breakfast!"

Mrs Binns flushed at the compliment and soon made herself comfortable.

"Do you know a gentleman living here called Alphonso Darling?" asked Frederick.

"A local man?" Mrs Binns narrowed her eyes, "The name does not sound at all familiar."

"As far as we can ascertain he is a stranger to the village," replied Frederick, "A foreign gentleman with a swarthy skin and a thick, guttural accent."

Mrs Binns shook her head and took a long gulp of tea. "No, no wait a minute," she cried, putting her cup down, "The gentleman up at Reeve's End. Do you remember the place, Mr Lawrence? Your uncle once rented it from Charlie Blain."

Lawrence nodded.

"Do go on," said Frederick, his heart racing in excitement.

"I don't know the man's name but Owen Blain, that is Charlie's son, said a foreign-looking man had plagued him to rent his crumbling mansion. Followed him night and day to get a decision. Terrible damp at Reeve's End and most of the rooms far from habitable!"

"And is he there now?" asked Frederick, clearing his plate.

"I saw Owen three days ago and he told me the man had insisted on paying twice over what he asked, so as to make sure he secured the place. What he does up there all day and all night Owen could not say. Come over from somewhere like Romania. No, I don't think that was it...I can't remember the exact country but somewhere far away that is similar."

Frederick looked at Lawrence and they both rose. "Mrs Binns, you have been more than helpful with your knowledge. If you can furnish us with directions to this place, just in case Lawrence does not remember, we will leave you in peace!"

The men left at once. Feeling replete and having obtained the directions for their mile walk, Frederick believed at last they were making progress.

"What will you say to Darling, should he be at home?" asked Lawrence, as they breasted the hill out of Scar's End.

"I have no idea," replied Frederick with total honesty, "I hope something will spring into my mind when the time comes."

"But should we not plan it?" asked the naturally more cautious Lawrence, panting as they reached the summit, "Otherwise we may make the man suspicious surely?"

Frederick stopped to consider the sense of this.

"I think we should question him on what he was doing on the moor that night. I mean, he saw Verity and did nothing to help her at all, apart from giving her the wrong directions to the village. Ask him if he saw anyone else on the moors that night. Tell him a lady was left in the dark in distress."

They were approaching the lofty dwelling now and its grim outline rose up against the January cold.

"It's a big place," murmured Frederick, "Far larger than Coombe Heights."

"I remember coming up here as a child," replied Lawrence, "It was with my father and he said the place gave him the creeps then, when it was reasonably sound, and not derelict as now."

They had instinctively stopped as though to summon up the courage to proceed. Even Frederick felt the eerie atmosphere it exuded and he was loath to go on.

"My legs seemed to have developed a mind of their own and are telling me they want to retreat," he told his companion, "But we must go on."

Soon the whole massive house front came into view, with a great deal of decay showing in the building's greying face. Windows grinned glassless smiles onto the tangle of moor that surrounded the place, and here and there, holes in the roof seemed like wounds in the house's head.

"It has not prospered with the passage of the years, that is for sure," murmured Lawrence, who remembered a far more uniform dwelling. Now mosses, lichens and even house plants, grew in crevices and whilst they looked, a number of tiles fell to the ground in the wind's blow.

"Part of it must be habitable, at least," answered Frederick, "Our friend must have a few rooms at the front or back that are free from decay. Let us go round to the side and see what becomes visible."

This they did, but the decay seemed universal, although round the back they noticed a kitchen window with boxes piled against it and a small lobby or outbuilding that looked sound.

"Maybe our friend has not had time to unpack," Frederick whispered.

The stables were at the back and the men found a handsome black charger, deep in straw, consuming a bucket of water.

"Ah. It seems our gentleman is at home then," concluded Lawrence, wondering where they should knock. A number of other stables were occupied with wooden boxes that on closer investigation appeared to be...

"Coffins!" cried Frederick, lowering his voice as the wind whipped the word away. He gained entrance to the two stables and found that some of the boxes were tightly screwed down but others were open. In the open ones earth and dirt, smelling strangely of decay, rested.

"A vampire haven," murmured Frederick, "There is no doubt now that our newcomer has something to do with the influx of the Undead to the region."

He had no sooner said that when he became conscious of a presence behind him. Luckily he had quit the stables and was just in the yard but even so both men jumped. The dark figure came forward and called out to them.

"Who are you and what is your business on my property? I rent this place now, so you are trespassers."

Frederick came forward.

"Peace, friend," he said in an affable tone, "We were in the area and called to ask you a few questions, concerning a woman you met on the moors the other night."

The dark figure came out of the shadows and Frederick was struck by his swarthy skin but vivid blue eyes. He was wearing a full length riding coat and was evidently on his way out somewhere judging by the cane he carried and the vermilion kerchief wrapped around the lower portion of his face. He sported a large, heavy-brimmed, black hat and Frederick noticed the glint of spurs on his dark trousers.

"Who says I was on the moors the other night?" came the voice, in a thick foreign tone.

"You met a woman - a lady I should say, who asked you for directions to Scar's End. I wondered if you saw anyone else that night."

The face relaxed into a smile, almost a laugh, which was beyond demonic. Visages like that were only meant to scowl and seethe, Frederick thought.

"Ah, now I am with you, gentlemen. The beauty on the footpath, lost in her reverie. I merely passed by on my way here and tried my best to furnish her with directions but I have been here mere days and my mind was not clear. I trust she made it home safely?"

"Eventually," replied Frederick, "But she had a nasty shock and is still far from well. I wondered if you saw any one else on the moor that evening?"

"As far as I recall, it was late afternoon and dusk coming down with the sparkle of frost," replied the foreigner, "Did I introduce myself gentlemen? Alphonso Darling, at your service!"

"You still have not answered our question," put in Lawrence.

"Ah, of course. We were lost in introductions. Perhaps if you gentlemen would tell me your names I might feel more obliged to assist you. I like to know who I am dealing with."

"Frederick, and Lawrence Grey," returned Frederick, anxious to keep his surname out of it in case rumours of his work had spread to this man's ears.

"Well, well, I am pleased to meet you." Alphonso came closer and shook hands with both men. Frederick found the whole experience repulsive. It was like touching wet and rotting fish.

"So now I will answer your question," said the man, stepping back a little. Frederick, who was in advance, caught the fetid and rotten stench of his breath. "No, nothing living appeared to me as I made my way back here and the beauty vanished, and if I failed to assist her in her plight then I am heartily sorry. I presume she has recovered from the experience?"

"Not quite," replied Frederick, "Bad dreams still assail her and nightmares too."

"Ah...she sounds like a tender flower and not one who should be wandering in January cold."

"It is February tomorrow," replied Lawrence.

"Why, so it is. How clever your friend is to remember! The days all seem the same to me but as I told you I have been here a mere couple of weeks."

"And may we ask what your business is here, Mr Darling?" returned Frederick.

"You may ask, sir, but I have no reason to tell you. Perhaps I should ask you what your business is in the locality first?"

"I am visiting my uncle here," replied Frederick, not taking his eyes off the foreigner, "But I am of English descent whereas you..."

"Are very definitely NOT!" came the loud reply, "Yes, I find the natives are not very friendly here. Worse than that, they are hostile, aggressive and suspicious I find. They desire to know my business and I desire they do not!"

"Sounds like you have something to hide in this old, decaying mansion, Mr Darling?"

"No more than the average man, Mr Grey. No more and no less."

"You are from Romania I believe?"

"Thereabouts. It is all the same to me – the soil I tread upon. You may say that. And now gentlemen, having answered your questions, I must leave you. I am anxious to meet the friend I came here for." He pushed past the men and approached a room just behind them where he obtained tack for his horse.

"I will bid you good day," he bowed "I would request you leave my property before I do. Let us just say, a peculiar whim of my character is not to leave strangers snooping whilst I am away. I wish the woman good health. I am not sure which of you possesses her, as you both seem

127

intoxicated by her, but then - as I remember - she was a beauty!"

Frederick motioned Lawrence to leave, at least for now. "Good day, Mr Darling. I hope your business, whatever it is, goes well this day," Lawrence called as they drew off but the figure vanished, and the men rounded the side of the house and took the path to the moor. They did not speak at first, as they waited to see if the horseman would overtake them and when he came, like a demon let out of hell, they watched him gallop off into the distance before discussing the visit.

"Well, that revealed a good bit about our friend anyway," commenced Frederick, as the sound of the hoof beats died on the cold air, "Coffins packed up with earth in them - presumably from Transylvania – the home of the original vampires. No doubt brought over here when Darling came. I doubt that is his real name anyway."

"So you think he is the Master?" asked Lawrence, breasting a hillock and drawing his coat around him, as the wind was bitter.

"Yes, unless he works for a bigger force, he is the adversary we now must destroy if we are to end this reign of terror in the village."

"So how will we do that?" questioned Lawrence, "I don't mean what will we use to despatch him, I know that, but how will we undertake it when Darling has the cunning of twenty vampires and there are just the two of us?"

"I haven't thought that far as yet, friend," replied Frederick, "There has to be a way. We need to watch his every movement but that would take an army of us and we are but two. I fear the gypsy camp will require our attention before too long."

"But will they let us back there when they dismiss our words as lies?"

"They will have to when things escalate, as they doubtless will. I am praying the gypsies have a change of heart."

His words were partly prophetic as, when they arrived at Frederick's lodgings, his landlady said a man had called a few minutes ago and, finding the men out, said he would return.

"I think he was one of those gypsies at Lea Woods," the lady told them, "There was a smell of rabbit stew about him such as I have smelt before on those travellers."

Frederick looked at Lawrence.

"It didn't take long," he murmured to his friend.

"Perhaps you would be so good as to make us both some tea whilst we wait for our visitor to return, Mrs Binns, please?"

"Yes, sir," she replied, "Due to the rather powerful odour of the visitor, I would be grateful if you would talk to him outside, please?"

"Leave him at the door and I will come down and see him," Frederick told her, hoping the news at the camp was not as grave as he suspected.

The knock came at last. Frederick hurried from his room and was halfway down the stairs before the door was opened.

"I'll take it from here," he called to Mrs Binns, who nodded her head in acknowledgement and went back to the kitchen.

"Trouble?" he asked the tall, thin gypsy youth who stood framed in the doorway.

"Yes, sir."

"We can talk about it as we walk, as I presume you require my attendance?"

"Please, sir. I was told to do everything in my power to get you to return with me."

Lawrence had joined them by then and the men threw on overcoats and donned hats. In a minute or so they were out in the cold air.

"So, what has happened?" asked Frederick, pulling his gloves on. The day had advanced and, with it, the temperature had dropped.

"It was last night, sir," began the youth, "My dad thought Joshua was better, it being his turn to watch him, and he seemed far quieter so we left him and slept. I mean he was tied down with every belt on the camp so he couldn't have

129

gotten anywhere. So the whole camp left him in the caravan and slept in the tents. It was the first sleep we'd had since that thing came and took Richard, so we needed it. Most slept like the dead, pardon the expression, but about 3 o'clock in the morning, I heard noises coming from the van. I jumped up and hurried over there and please the Holy Mother protect me from what I saw-"

"What did you see?" asked Frederick, observing the lad was becoming hysterical and he breathed as fast as a kitten. "Wait a minute! Stop and get your breath, recover your composure and tell us slowly and calmly, if you can. It is very important we know all the details."

The lad was clearly overcome and he knelt down for a minute and struggled to control his feelings. His breath slowed a little and he looked up at the two men with scared green eyes.

"I saw our Richard bending over our Joshua and he was biting him on the neck. I screamed or shouted, I am not sure which, and Richard looked up and his eyes blazed at me and blood dribbled from his open mouth. Sharp, white teeth, as long as the bear's I saw in a picture book and white as snow. It was just for a second, maybe a few, and then the whole camp seemed with me, wakened from their slumbers," He gulped for air at this point and Frederick put a comforting hand on his shoulder.

"What of Joshua?" Lawrence asked, in concern.

"Dead, mister. As dead as a doornail. The thing had drunk his life blood out of him and you can't live with empty veins, sir!"

Frederick and Lawrence looked at each other. At least they knew now what they faced and it could hardly be any worse.

When they arrived at the gypsy camp, a loud wailing greeted their ears. The youth, whose name was Albert, said he would fetch his father, who turned out to be the uncle of the dead boys. Their father, it appeared, was too lost in shock to speak.

Daniel Enderby shook hands with the vampire hunters and his fingers shook.

"My brother should have listened to you," he said in an apologetic voice, "However, his wife is ruled by the Bible and it rubs off, you see. What you suggested was almost blasphemy to her."

"This is no time for recriminations," Frederick replied, "Our help is still on offer should you need it."

"We need it more than ever it appears," Daniel told him, "Tell me the worst. Will both my nephews turn into – those things."

"Vampires," finished Lawrence, "And, regretfully, the answer is yes."

Daniel sat down heavily on a stool.

"We have scarcely buried one and now we have to inter another," he whispered, almost to himself.

"I expect your brother told you what we have to do, to stop this I mean," Frederick said gently.

"Yes - mutilate the body."

"It is the only way," Lawrence told him, "The boys are already dead and beyond hope for this earth anyway but don't you want them to shine in glory with the saints? Or they will be left, forever wandering, as the Undead, suffering and lusting after blood?"

Daniel nodded his head.

"Please, do what you need to in order to end this nightmare for us," he replied, "The whole camp and I know there is no other way but what you suggest. We may not like it but we recognise it as the truth now."

"We shall need your help though," Frederick told him, "You must love them both as much as you did in life and never, ever let that love waver, even for an instant. That will restore them to the paths of heaven."

Thus, a few minutes later, Frederick found himself facing the whole camp, some twenty people and a few children, all sad, grave and silent. Grey, ashen faces were turned towards him with tears running down both old and young cheeks. He

131

felt suddenly nervous. What if he failed them? But the power of love was unfailing and he knew that.

"Friends," he cried, summoning up his flagging spirits and glancing at Lawrence who stood by his side for support. "Friends – you have had a tragic time since we saw you last and, although we feel your pain, we cannot stop it without your help. How many of you loved those boys with your heart, mind and soul?" All twenty hands went up and the older children who understood also raised hesitant hands. "How many of you still love those boys, even though their earthly bodies are still and silent?"

Not a hand wavered. All twenty stayed up.

"Your faith is strong, friends, and I praise you for that. It will get those boys to the gates of heaven, for sure."

He briefly explained about the vampire's psyche and how love worked on a different vibration to the one they existed on.

"Their vibration is low – at base level, but love is so high and pure and unadulterated, they cannot stand it. With love they are dead before the stake and mallet," Lawrence now raised those tools... "hits them. The blow is merely our insurance that they are gone."

There was a gasp of horror at the idea and one lad shouted out,

"I heard you have to separate the head from the body and fill the mouth with garlic!"

"There is no need for that any more," Frederick told him, talking louder as voices were raised, "Not with love. I tell you, friends, we can have them at the door of heaven ready for St Peter to let them in!"

However, some of the voices of the older ones were still raised in anger at the proposed mutilation of the bodies but, just then, the small crowd parted and a middle-aged woman made her way through. She walked straight up to the two men. She was strikingly beautiful and had the look of Verity about her eyes. The raised voices were lowered and then the whole group fell silent.

132

The gypsy flung back her dark mane of hair and in a clear voice she said,

"I am the mother of those boys and I turned these men away once, thinking what they said violated everything in my favourite book. Yet the Bible has failed me, religion has failed me and taken my boys far away. They are dead and yet, they are Undead. I still pray to my God but He tells me to trust these men. They have returned to us through the goodness of their hearts and I prayed...I prayed so hard for a sign and these men are the answer. We must do what they tell us! If not, friends, how many more of us will die in this terrible way and then wander the earth for eternity, seeking to destroy our fellow men?"

A ripple of something like understanding went round the group, like the murmur of wind in growing wheat, and Frederick relaxed a little. He had them all on side now.

CHAPTER ELEVEN

"We have to forget about Alphonso until we get this sorted out," Lawrence said later, as they sat alone in one of the brightly painted gypsy caravans.

"Leave the Master to his musings, eh?" Frederick replied. "I feel our loyalties are here and, until we send the boys to meet their Maker, Darling will have to be left to his own devices. Doubtless he is adding to our troubles as we speak."

"There may be a way the gypsies can help us with him when the situation here is resolved," Lawrence continued pensively, "Some of these men are excellent poachers and hunters."

Frederick agreed.

"Yes, certainly they could live by tickling the trout out of the streams and bagging a few hares or pheasants," he acknowledged.

"We need to make use of their cunning and guile. Could they not watch Alphonso's place for us? After all, if they were seen on the moors they would just be snaring rabbits, as generations of their ancestors have done."

"Hmm, the local gamekeeper may not be too happy with that," Frederick admitted.

"Well, in truth, they won't be snaring anything but Darling, hopefully of course. They can tell us his movements and if he has any more strange deliveries."

"Like the coffins full of earth?"

"Exactly."

"It is an excellent plan, if we can trust them to do the job. Some of them are working on the farm for the next two weeks but not all of them."

"I think, resolve the problem here first and then broach it with them when they are exuding gratitude for our work?"

Frederick gave a hollow laugh.

"Mutilate two young bodies and they will be eternally grateful? Oh, the irony of it!"

"Well, it is far better than what would befall them were we to turn and walk away."

Night came swiftly and with it came freezing temperatures, so Lawrence and Frederick huddled over the fire the gypsies had lit and ate rabbit stew and drank mead but at 7 o'clock in the morning, when a faint glow appeared in the sky, nothing had occurred. All was quiet.

February was here and, as the old rhyme stated, as the days lengthened the cold strengthened. The gypsies had buried both boys now and an agreement was reached with the elders to stake the bodies, whilst the immediate family sent as much love as they could muster.

"We have mourned our losses, performed our traditions and had our time of grief," said the grandfather of the boys, "True, it has been quiet but in that stillness, our despair for the future has returned and the sooner it is done the better for us all. We all give permission for the graves to be dug up before the Undead predate again. We have been lucky in the peace but I know it will not always be this way."

Frederick and Lawrence bowed their heads.

"It will be done with all the reverence and love we can rally," Frederick declared.

"Our rituals have been performed to the best of our abilities and, now, we just want them safe in the arms of Jesus and this, sad though it is, seems to be the only way," the grandfather acknowledged.

Frederick went to visit Verity and tell her what was going to happen. She had gained composure and health in the last couple of days and he was delighted to see her looking so well.

"So, the boys have not been seen since that dreadful night?" she asked, "Both of them, Frederick? Oh, this is truly shocking - two lives cut short, two children dead."

"Undead, Verity."

"Well, removed from this life anyway. Will you really mutilate a child?"

"I have to if I am to restore them to the peace their families crave for them. Otherwise, they are set to wander the world as parasites for eternity."

"It seems so cruel and heartless."

"In the eyes of the unbeliever it is but what they could do is far, far worse than our ministrations. Why, I have heard in some foreign countries, if they suspect a body to be that of a vampire they totally dismember it and strew the parts over many miles, to fool the bloodsuckers."

Verity shivered. This whole business was so distasteful and every day it seemed to get worse.

"Are we really winning the war against these creatures?" she asked now.

Frederick looked thoughtful.

"We shall win the final battle and that is what counts. But, believe me, it will be far worse than this, Verity."

Later that day both men went out to Bollard's Hill. The sky was just beginning to darken and a furious wind hurled spent leaves against the walkers' faces.

Frederick carried his Bible, prayer book, stake and mallet, and Lawrence had phials of Holy Water and his family prayer book. Both men had heavy hearts. There was something additionally disturbing about children as vampires and Frederick said, to his knowledge, he had never had to perform these rituals on brothers like this.

"My youngest was a 12 year old girl, just north of Lincoln," he told Lawrence, "This feels far more tragic."

"We must view it as taking them from the torture of the Undead and restoring them to the sight of heaven, at last," Lawrence replied.

The gypsy camp was quiet and peaceful when they arrived. The men had returned from their labour on the farm and the women from their work in the fields. Some of the elders were cooking a meal and two fires had been lit. There were four beautifully painted caravans and to the largest of these the two men now repaired.

"We are come, as promised," Frederick told the gypsy elder, "Darkness crowds the sky now, so our work can begin. Will you show us where you have buried the boys?"

The elder called forth the parents and they came, carrying Bibles, and Frederick could see the glint of crosses about their necks.

"You are protected," he told them, "However, before we begin this sad affair we must pray."

When that was over, lanterns were lit and the four players in this tragic game travelled to where the boys had been laid to rest. It was a calm night now, and the wind seemed to have abated. The trees shook their empty branches every so often, but other than that silence reigned. A few very early windflowers and some burnished, copper leaves graced the grave.

"My sons both loved searching the meadows and fields for these flowers," said the mother, in almost a whisper. She moved as though in a trance and her eyes were full of tears but they were full of love also, and Frederick felt hope move within him.

"It took us three days to find these fading blossoms so we could put something living on the grave. We found them in a sheltered nook on the far side of the wood. The wind had not blown in upon the resting seeds and what little sun we have had these past weeks had nourished them and they had grown..."

More prayers were said and then Lawrence and Frederick began to dig up the grave. Lawrence sprinkled the ground with Holy Water to protect them and noticed how the liquid hissed and steamed when it hit the soil. Another piece of proof they were disturbing a vampire grave.

Then suddenly, out of the shadows of approaching night, two figures ducked under the trees and came closer.

"My boys! My boys!" cried the mother, holding out her hand to them but her husband grabbed her arm.

"They are not your boys," he growled, "Do not go to them!"

Frederick leapt from the grave.

"They have pre-empted us and risen," he murmured. The two small figures came resolutely onward and, as light from the rising moon and the lanterns fell on their faces, the mother recoiled in shock. Red eyes, with the refulgence of

137

the Devil in them and huge teeth falling from mouths that already exuded a trickle or two of blood.

"They have been feasting on animals here, no doubt," Lawrence whispered, climbing out of the hole to join his friend, "Get ready, Frederick."

The smaller boy put out his hand to his mother. It dripped blood and a portion of animal skin adhered to the fingers. She shrieked in horror and turned away.

"Please, help us," cried Joshua in his own tone, although his appearance was so different, "These men have come to destroy us. See, we are alive and you, Mother and Father, may join us. Just one bite...one bite..."

"I love you, boys! I love you, boys!" their mother called, in response to the pleading. Her hand gripped her husband's arm and she stayed strong and never moved. Both children grimaced and turned away to avoid the high vibration.

"No, no," spat Richard, the elder one, through clenched teeth, "No, do not speak of such a vile emotion. We do not want that as it will not satisfy us. We need blood!"

"And I love you both too," from the father, "I love you to eternity and back. I will always love you. We both love you. Love, love, love. Take it boys as it comes tumbling over you!"

Both of the boys were on their knees now, writhing as if in agony. The parents looked away and could not bear to see their offspring in such pain. Yet still they sent out the love, pure, high, unadulterated, to cut off the low, base energy of the vampire. Alien to a bloodsucker's soul it had the power to suffocate, choke and asphyxiate the evil out of them.

Whilst they were thus distracted, the men sprung into action.

"Keep the vibration flowing!" called Frederick to the parents as he raised the stake and took aim with the mallet, "With as much love as my heart can muster, I do this thing. I send you to heaven and drain the evil out of you!" He struck perfectly and silence flowed.

When the older boy saw what fate beheld his brother, he set up a hideous wailing and tried to escape but Lawrence was ready for him. With the love choking the evil out of him Richard was already dying.

"Find peace, take peace, eternal peace," prayed Frederick and raised the stake once more.

It was daylight again. The four people had kept a strange vigil over the bodies of the two boys and now, with the return of the light, they could be buried again. This time they would not rise to torment and drain the rest of the gypsies. They were at peace. Their bodies had returned to the innocent faces of children and the parents hugged them and touched their soft cheeks and closed eyes. The smiles on their pale lips were now those of perfect peace. The fetid breath, the red eyes and the huge teeth had faded as soon as the stake was driven home, and in their place, the lighter features of children. Thus do cherubims look, at Abraham's bosom.

When the light was firmly established in the sky the men left the camp, knowing that the gypsies were anxious to inter the bodies for the last time. This time there would be no mourning or weeping or wailing, a far greater sorrow had been prevented and the boys stood, in each gypsy's eye anyway, at the gates of heaven. Frederick prayed St Peter would feel mercy and let them in. He felt tired and stale, drained now of any emotion and he knew Lawrence, as the elder man, was exhausted too. Half of his mind wanted to go and see Verity but his body craved sleep and solitude and he planned to see her when he woke. Everything was far too raw now, and he might say the wrong thing and upset her. Besides, she would be asleep and he had no desire to wake up the household. He could still see the red eyes of the boys coming through the darkness and he could still hear the drip of blood from their hands, still smell the fetid stench of their breath and feel the clammy, fish-like coldness of their skin. He shook his head, as if to dispel the image. With luck, sleep would wash it away.

How many more do we have to pursue and kill - or should that be un-kill, since they were Undead - he wondered, as he followed Lawrence back to the village through the cold, first light. The Master and Verity's uncle would be the worst.

They were both too tired to make much conversation and at Frederick's lodgings they parted.

"Once sleep has refreshed me, I will go to see Verity," said Frederick, in a weary voice.

"It is not over yet, my friend," Lawrence reminded him, "And I fear the greatest test is yet to come."

"Alphonso," murmured Frederick, "Yes, you are right."

"There is Verity's uncle too," continued Lawrence, "For though he may not put up much of a fight, there is that link by blood."

"I doubt Verity will mourn his loss as we hurl him from the ranks of the Undead. They were not close in life."

"True." Lawrence did not sound very convinced, "I will leave you now, friend," he said, straightening up, "Do not forget the woman, for she is still at large. No word of her, except Verity hearing her conversation with the vampire who we presume was Verity's uncle."

"More sheep killed, which could have been her," Frederick told him but he felt his brain was closing down with exhaustion.

"Alphonso has to be our next target," he finished. "Kill the Master and the rest will scatter."

Six hours later, and refreshed by a sleep that was predominantly restful, Frederick took himself to Verity's. However, to his surprise, the woman was not at home.

"She took herself off about ten o'clock this morning," Liddy told him, "She would not tell me where she was going but remarked that she would be back for luncheon, if I delayed it till two."

Frederick looked at his watch. It wanted some twenty minutes to two now.

"May I wait?" he asked the maid.

"Of course, sir. I will make you some tea and add enough for your appetite at luncheon."

"Thank you, Liddy."

The fire was made up in the parlour and Frederick sank into the settle to await Verity's return. He was just dozing off when he heard the front door bang and Verity's voice in the hallway.

She came into the parlour, remarking on the coldness of the day. Frederick got up and took her hand.

"I was worried where you were," he began.

Verity raised her eyebrows.

"I took a carriage out to Bollard's Hill," she said simply. Now it was Frederick's turn to raise his eyebrows.

"I wanted to see the boys' grave," she qualified, "After all, it was my uncle who killed them as well you know Frederick..."

"You are not responsible!"

"Nevertheless, after what I heard on the moors, I had to pay my respects."

"But the gypsies?"

"They greeted me cordially. I said I was a friend of yours."

"What did you do?"

"I was up at the break of dawn and found some early flowers and some fragrant herbs in the garden, to anoint the grave."

"It was very dangerous, Verity!"

"How? They sleep easy in their graves now, do they not?"

"Yes, but your uncle is at large and so is Alphonso."

"It is daylight, Frederick. I will not stir from this place at night, that I promise you. My heart feels more at ease now. I have every faith in your ability to finish off what you started but you must allow me my feminine touches!"

"It was a lovely thought, Verity, and it does you credit but I am concerned for your safety."

"Do not be, dear Frederick. I will do as you say from now on, I promise."

Liddy knocked then to say luncheon was ready and their talk was shelved for food but as they sat in the parlour enjoying beverages after the meal, Frederick explained his plans.

"It seems Alphonso is definitely the kingpin in all of this. Possibly the Master, as we call him. The coffins full of earth confirm this, and his very strange demeanour too. To a certain extent, he controls the vampires in this region..."

"You think there are a lot more to find then?" interrupted Verity.

Frederick shook his head.

"The other maiden definitely and your uncle but, hopefully, that will be it."

"So, how do you propose to ensnare Alphonso? I cannot see him submitting as easily as it seems the two boys did."

Frederick rubbed his chin thoughtfully.

"No," he replied, at length, "He has been immured for centuries possibly, in the Undead's power. The boys were fresh and new to the eternity of vampirism, so they had little power but he will...I am not too sure at present. Lawrence said he will go back to the gypsy camp and try to persuade some of them to watch Alphonso for us. The older ones do not work in the fields and they could do it."

"But are they not on their way soon?" asked Verity.

"They have another ten days or so on the farm," Frederick told her, "A week should confirm his movements and see exactly what he is up to."

"Gypsies are known for their stealth," Verity acknowledged, thinking of her own experiences.

"Exactly. If they were seen, they could simply be setting snares on the moorland around his place. I think he has bigger issues to deal with than a couple of travellers snaffling a bit of free food. I do not think they will arouse his suspicions. At least, I hope not. But Lawrence, as a local man, is better at dealing with that than I am. I have done my best for them but they still view me with suspicion."

"I have followed it up with a touch of compassion, I hope."

They both lapsed into an easy silence and then Frederick rose, put his empty cup on the tray, and said he must go.

142

Exhaustion seemed to be eating into him again and he craved more sleep.

God knows what will be sent for us to deal with over the next few days, he thought.

He went home – or what he thought of as home – but could not formulate any plan concerning Alphonso. Kill the Master and the rest will scatter, like chaff in the wind, he thought. However, before they do, we will kill them too.

He must have been dozing, as suddenly he found Lawrence was standing over him. He came to with a jolt.

"Sorry," he murmured, "I didn't hear a knock. I'm so drained mentally and physically. It's one devil of a case."

Lawrence sat down.

"I've got the gypsies on side," he told Frederick, "They are going to watch Alphonso. It is only a mile from their place and to a gypsy, even an elderly one, that is nothing. They are going up there now and will report back to me this evening."

"You're a good man, Lawrence," Frederick replied gratefully.

The gypsy, true to his word, visited Lawrence later that day and reported Alphonso's comings and goings.

"More coffins delivered, sir," he said, fingering his cap a little nervously, "Couldn't see what was in them but the carriage only had four and seemed weighed down and the old horse really struggled."

"What time was that?" asked Lawrence, preparing to write it down to tell Frederick who was sleeping for a few hours.

"About two, in the afternoon that is, sir. In fact, the driver had to knock many times, and it seemed Mr Darling had only just risen as his hair was all over the place and he brushed sleep from his eyes."

"Nothing before the coffins came?"

"No, sir. Nor anything after either. 'Twas as quiet as the grave, pardoning my way of speaking. Not a soul about."

"You have done very well, Robert, and I am grateful. Can you resume your watch from nine o'clock tomorrow morning?"

"Yes, sir. Of course, sir. And report back to you again in the early evening?"

"Yes, Robert, please. Frederick and I will take over now. We will have some money for you tomorrow. A guinea to help your struggling family!"

"Thank you, sir. We have fourteen days apparently, before we leave but I will watch for you until then, should I be needed of course. My back is too bad for fieldwork now, sir, but a little watching and a rabbit or two for the pot is a pleasant day's work!"

An hour later Frederick and Lawrence met up and armed themselves with Holy Water and their faithful crosses. Taking a slatted lantern they set off for Alphonso's. It was pitch dark with very little moonlight, so they had to walk round by the old and now deserted turnpike road, thus adding miles to their journey but protecting themselves from quicksands and bogs.

"You say more coffins have arrived?" queried Frederick, as they set out, "There were six there I believe when we last visited."

"Correct. Four more came yesterday afternoon. Apart from that, no activity to report."

"I wonder what our friend is up to?" Frederick mused, as they walked.

"I have a feeling we are going to find out very soon; if not this very night," Lawrence replied.

"Unless we can destroy him before then," his friend replied hopefully.

A light was burning in the mansion when they arrived but silence prevailed. The outbuildings were securely locked and bolted and there was no way of gaining admittance without tools and brute strength. The men heard dogs baying and howling and their blood chilled.

"He is well protected," sighed Frederick, "He will not be an easy man to get near."

"We may have to entrap him somehow," whispered Lawrence, as the dogs yowled their message to the night sky, "He is not going to fall on his sword any time soon and, judging by what he is accumulating, he expects a visitor who will spread the vampire curse far and wide."

"Desperate times call for desperate measures," Frederick told him, "I may need to offer myself as bait. I have done so before, of course. I cannot see a vat of stale blood attracting the likes of Alphonso!"

"No – nor Verity's uncle either. I sense he may be higher in the vampire hierarchy than the woman anyway!"

"We still have one of those at large, slaughtering our sheep for a mouthful of blood. She'll not come for the vats, were she dry for months."

Silence came down like frost and hit them but somehow it made it even more eerie. Then abruptly, the crunching of feet on gravel round the front of the house announced a visitor. The men were at the back but they could hear the dragging steps clearly on the sharp, cold air. It was a little after eleven and starting to freeze.

"Someone is coming," whispered Frederick, "I will creep up and try to ascertain who it is. You stay here," and he inched his way forward, keeping to the shadows. By degrees he got to the house front and heard a knock and then the great door falling inwards as the call was answered. The dogs went mad but a single shout silenced them. Alphonso obviously had them eating out of the palm of his hand. Frederick clung to the wall and listened to the conversation taking place.

"Four more arrived today and another four are expected tomorrow. Our Master will hit England later this month and we will furnish a royal reception for him. So sad Rose has been destroyed as he would have loved her young, yielding flesh."

It was clearly Alphonso's voice. Frederick listened intently. So, who would answer him? A man's voice came back to him from the darkness.

"But they are destroying us! Do you not realise that? Rose was taken and now Fancy hides her face for fear the vampire

145

hunter finds her. He lured her to my old place with the blood that I bought for the crops but it is stale and rancid now and we need fresh blood. Fresh blood!"

"Silence, you fool!" shouted Alphonso, making the dogs howl yet again, "Do you not have the sheep on the moors for fodder every night and you had two small boys found wandering at Bollard's Hill, did you not?"

"Yes, and the vampire hunter pierced them both and sent them to meet their maker before they could join us! Ah, how sweet the young ones are with their blood red eyes and sharp teeth!"

"Do not complain to me! Do not interrupt me again. I am your Master and you report to me, even though you control the women!"

"Only one left, Mr Darling, and she hangs up in Cliffe Woods, sucking the blood from squirrels and rats, for fear of encountering the slayer! We cannot get our teeth anywhere near this hunter, he is surrounded by garlic and Holy Water and much worse still, LOVE!"

"Do not prattle on at me in this way, as if I am responsible. Have you not got the whole village at your disposal, not to mention the travellers passing through?"

"The villagers are wise to us, sir, and keep every door and window closed after dark and we must keep away from the glare of daylight."

"The Master will sort this out when he comes. Even my powers stale before his. You must trust and you must be patient. A few more days and he will be with us, and the message will go far and wide. For now I can do nothing. I have to feed too. The slayer has no real or lasting power compared to our Master."

"He has Holy Water to burn our skin and the force of God is on his side," bewailed the man.

"Bah! We have the armies of Satan at our beck and call! How can he take on the might of hell and win?"

"Before I met your kind, when I was in my earthly body, I feared the Devil and worshipped God. I made myself into a hermit for his holy cause."

"And yet, with one bite you are hurtling down to the Underworld and the promise of eternity as the Undead then? You have forever to ponder this so do not waste my time now. I tell you, once the true Master sees this hunter, the man will be one of us in an instant!"

"My niece keeps me away night and day with her suffocating affection! Night after night she sends such love that my soul is literally rotting with goodness. It nauseates me. I am revolted and sickened by it."

"Hmm. It seems the vampire hunter has taught her well. He learnt how to destroy us with the love vibration when all else had failed him and he was backed into a corner. He will pay for that. They all will. Go find yourself a sheep, my friend, and be grateful for that. You could be stone dead and singing vile songs of praise and glory to God. Be Undead and enjoy the promise of eternity! Goodnight!" And with that the door was firmly shut.

The dogs started again, as though to warn the visitor he needed to leave promptly and the interview was over. He saw the sense in this as, even in the vampire world, class matters, and soon his dragging footsteps faded on the still, night air.

Frederick returned to Lawrence and relayed exactly what he had heard.

"So, there is no doubt this was Verity's uncle? Richard, I think she said his name was in an earlier conversation."

"This woman who is called Fancy – the one we still seek. Any news of her?"

"Terrified out of her wits after seeing us dispatch her friend to God's throne and holed up in Cliffe Woods."

"Ah yes - that is barely a mile from the village. Sounds like she could be a sitting target there, as they are neither large nor inaccessible."

"Exactly. I propose we go there at first light and see if we can track her down and send her on her way as she sleeps. Then there is just Richard and Alphonso, of course."

"Mmm, leaving the worst till last and at any minute they could attack someone and the vampire population here

147

would be doubled! Thus, the chain of the Undead could make fresh links and it is for us to break them."

"Sadly, yes. However, our main worry seems to be this Absolute Master who seeks entry to the country in a few days. It appears he has more power than any other vampire we have ever encountered."

"He is dependent on Darling to get here then?"

"It seems so."

Lawrence fell silent. His face was pensive and he chewed his lip whilst trying to formulate a plan.

"I think we need to put every inch of our strength into destroying Darling," he said, at length, "It sounds as though, if we can do that, the Promised One will be left high and dry, so our shores may not be an option for him. We are not sure how long it is before he arrives, either."

"A few days was the phrase uttered," Frederick told him.

"It may even take more than a few days to ensnare Alphonso but once we have him dispatched to hell the other two will be easy."

Frederick nodded.

"Darling knows me and would, I believe, take a great delight in draining my feeble body of blood. Therefore, I shall offer myself up as bait in a trap and draw him in," He rolled up his sleeve to reveal a long scar on his forearm.

"I got that in Scotland, a year ago, trapping a vampire in the glens," he told his friend, "It is an old wound but I would gladly open it up again, or add a brother to it, in order to ensnare Alphonso. Fresh blood. He will not be able to resist it."

CHAPTER TWELVE

After sleeping and bathing, Frederick went to see Verity, who had fully recovered from her ordeal and was anxious for news. She worried about Frederick and, to a lesser extent, Lawrence, being near to a man who she classed as evil. His cold, blue eyes – orbs of steel, reflecting his shadow in eternity – still haunted her at night and she could not even retire until Liddy assured her every blind in the room was drawn down and the windows secured.

"What news last night?" asked Verity, when Frederick had settled himself by the fire and Liddy had bustled away to make tea, "I – I don't like you being near that man and that is the plain, honest truth, Frederick. What if he were to find you? Surely he could smell your blood?"

Frederick avoided her eyes. He knew he could not tell her he was prepared to be a sacrifice at the vampire altar in order to trap this dangerous man. Verity would foresee the worst and have him as one of the Undead before the sun rose.

He was glad of Liddy's entrance to divert her mistress and it was a few minutes before the subject was broached again. "We have to destroy this man no matter what it takes, Verity," he said at last, when a few mouthfuls of tea had revived him, "He is the kingpin here and through him, a new evil will enter the country and spread its malignant wings over us all. My power may not be strong enough to contain this."

Verity looked rather shocked.

"So, how do you propose to destroy this man?" she asked, fixing her dark eyes on his face.

Frederick took another cake.

"These are exceptionally fine, Verity, I must say," he replied, biting into the sweet treat.

"Frederick, you know as well as I do, that Liddy has one recipe and one recipe only for her cakes, one which her mother gave her, and she judges that to be the finest in existence. They are always the same and not one more pinch of spice will she add, despite me producing my grandmother's recipe which is different but just as good. Let us leave the cakes and get back to the matter in hand."

Frederick put the remains of the cake on his plate and deposited it on the table by the fire. He had the grace to look a little guilty.

"I -I am not sure as yet," he muttered, "I have the vague beginnings of a plan but no definite outline."

Verity nodded.

"Good," she replied, "In that respect I am glad, as it makes it easier for me to say what I have to say. I have thought it through, Frederick, for many a night when sleep eluded me. Whatever you say, my soul must take some of the blame for this deplorable situation. He was my uncle after all."

Frederick tried to interrupt but Verity held up her hand to silence him and continued,

"It doesn't matter what you say, Frederick, I feel beholden to the village to make some sort of sacrifice," Frederick shivered at the word as, was it not what he planned to do? Verity carried on defiantly,

"You refused to let me help you at the crossroads. You would have refused to let me accompany you to Alphonso's, had I asked - that I know - but you cannot refuse me this. You have told me today how desperate you are to destroy this man, the 'kingpin' you called him, as he seeks to usher in a new kind of evil to our world, one that you may not be able to stop. Desperate times, Frederick, desperate times. Therefore, I will do what I did before and go out on the moors at night,"

"Never!" from Frederick.

"I will go out onto the moors at night," repeated Verity, in a louder voice, "I will knock on his door and profess myself lost and unwell. He will not refuse a damsel in distress when he smells my blood."

"Never!" from Frederick again, "Besides which, he has a pack of wolves in his house that could rip you from limb to limb."

Verity shook her head.

"You really think he is going to let those curs have me? Waste all that fresh, young blood, Frederick? He will want me all to himself!"

Frederick stood up.

"This is preposterous!" he spat, "Lawrence would never allow it! It is madness!"

"How come?" replied Verity calmly, "You need to destroy the man fast and he needs what I have...blood."

"It is out of the question," Frederick told her, "It is the scheme of a mad woman!"

"Surely you insult me with those words!" Verity came back, pretending to be vexed.

"How can I protect you if you throw yourself to him?"

"Who said I was going to? I will draw him onto the moorland with me, to help find some lost but sentimentally valuable trinket."

"You seriously believe he will fall for that?"

"Yes. More than any plot you concoct to entrap him. Why, the whole village knows you as the vampire slayer and Alphonso does too, so he will be wary of any contact with you. But ME? I saw the lust for me in his cold, blue eyes and I can see that you and Lawrence need to be waiting, ready to destroy him, but it is me who needs to draw him into this trap. My finger will have been pierced by the pin of a brooch I own, an heirloom, that will do perfectly for this game. I will draw him away from the house and right onto your path!"

Frederick struck his forehead.

"This is insane," he said, beginning to walk up and down, "It can't be done. He could bite as soon as he sees and smells the blood."

"He could – but he won't. I will have the wound covered by my handkerchief and just give him a small sniff of fresh blood. I will beg him to accompany me with a lantern, to find the heirloom, and then declare I am come over faint and need to rest at his. He will be as weak as a kitten when he knows that."

Jet chose to stand up and meow at that point when he heard the kitten reference. Frederick nodded his head at the cat's intervention.

"You do right, little fellow, to disapprove of your mistress's plan. You are on my side I see."

"On the contrary, Frederick, he backs me up with his voice and besides, he is as reliable as a clock striking the hour when his food is due. Ah, here is Liddy, with his dish of raw meat," she murmured, as a knock came at the door.

Frederick sat down again and watched the cat consume his meal in silence. When every piece had gone and Jet was solemnly washing his face he said,

"You have shocked me to the core, Verity. I want no part in this."

Verity settled herself down again.

"So, tell me, Frederick, how do you propose to destroy the man? From what you tell me the Absolute Master is due any day and then, such a can of worms is opened in our country that events will soon spiral totally out of control. Must we all be bitten in our beds?"

Trying to stay calm, Frederick explained his plan again, to offer himself up for bait, wounded and bleeding.

"Alphonso has far more animosity for you than for me, Frederick. He may see you as a meal to be consumed at once, such is his hatred for you, but with me...I am a delicacy to be cherished and salivated over!"

"Don't say that, Verity! It sounds obscene!"

"Admit then that success is far more likely with me on the fishing rod!"

Frederick argued a little more but saw he was not going to sway her. Finally, Verity agreed to see what Lawrence thought of the plan.

She called on Lawrence soon after Frederick had gone, giving the man time to reach his lodgings first and then setting off. To Liddy she said nothing more than that she was going out.

"Where to, miss, if I may be so bold as to ask?" enquired Liddy, her mind thinking back to the last time her mistress

had absented herself, "You must be back before nightfall, after what happened a few days ago, I worry so."
Verity pulled on her gloves.
"Really, Liddy, you do not need to be concerned. I am only off to the village!"
"That's as may be, miss, but you know what goes on there after dark. Mr Frederick said to watch you closely."
"Did he indeed, Liddy? Well, you can consider yourself relieved of those duties."
"Maybe I should accompany you, miss, just to put Mr Frederick's mind at rest? Unless of course you are off to visit him?"
"He only left here half an hour ago, Liddy, did he not? However, seeing as you are prying – no, I am not calling on Frederick."

Liddy was exasperated that silence now ensued and her mistress was not going to volunteer any further information. She tried again.
"Really, miss, I do not know what Mr Frederick would say."
"Then seeing it is ME who pays your wages, you do not have to worry. Please remain here and look after the house," Verity continued with her preparations to quit the place.
"You ask far too many questions, Liddy. Were anyone to overhear your views they would wonder who is maid and who is mistress," Verity was determined to see Lawrence in relative secrecy and gain his support for her plan.

When she was near his house she pulled her hood tight about her head and was glad of the February chill that meant she could easily hide her identity. Luck was with her and she saw the very man she sought, at the window ahead of her. She raised her hand in greeting and he moved to the door to admit her.

He expressed surprise that she had ventured out but was cut short by her question, asking if Frederick was with him. "No," he said, "I have not seen him. Have you two fallen out?"
Verity handed over her coat and gloves.

"Not exactly," she murmured, "Certainly, we have had a difference of opinion over something and I seek your advice most urgently."

"Before Frederick calls to try and get me to take his side, you mean?"

Verity smiled. Lawrence was very astute and she admired him for that quality. She waited until Lawrence had invited her into his sitting room and all was quiet and then she tried again.

"I have come up with a plan whereby we can destroy Alphonso," she began eagerly.

Lawrence frowned.

"So Frederick does not like this plan I take it?"

Verity raised her eyebrows.

"THAT is an understatement, if ever I heard one," she continued.

Lawrence, remembering his manners, ushered her into a chair and offered tea which she refused, as she was anxious to get on with her story.

"In truth, I cannot be long," she admitted, when she was seated comfortably, "If she could, Liddy would have followed me here, so keen was she to find out my mission."

It was Lawrence's turn to smile at that.

"Your maid sees and hears many things," he acknowledged.

"Too many for my liking," replied Verity, tossing her head with vague annoyance, "However, my plan, Lawrence. Please hear me out. Frederick jumped down my throat scarce before I had finished the first sentence!"

Lawrence sat back and gave her his full attention. During her speech he neither batted an eye nor raised an eyebrow, so she had no clue as to how he had received it. He steepled his long, thin fingers and blew upon them pensively.

"My dear Verity, your plan does you credit, it does indeed, BUT..."

"Does there have to be a 'but', Lawrence?" Verity interjected.

"Yes, my dear, I believe there has to be, as the plan has one fatal flaw. It is too dangerous."

"You are so in tune with Frederick!" Verity flashed back, "Can you not see that it would work?"

"I would certainly acknowledge its chance of success, if it were carefully planned, but there is a strong chance you could lose your life as well."

"That is a risk I am willing to take and, to be honest, I have no fears, providing you and Frederick are in close proximity."

There was a brief silence and then Verity continued. "I have every confidence I can capture Alphonso's attention, whereby he forgets all else, by using my blood and my womanly wiles," she said, "I have every confidence too, that you and Frederick can protect me and come to my aid when I need it. Most of all, I have every confidence that you can destroy this ghoul, once I have lured him away from his house," She looked triumphant.

"There, Lawrence, I have won you over, so will you now shake on it so we have a deal?" She leant forward and extended her hand.

However the man refused to shake.

"What Frederick would say were I to approve this madness, I do not know," replied Lawrence, shaking his head.

"Time is clearly not on our side," continued Verity, "Madness or not, do the pair of you have another idea you can put forward then?"

"Yes, Frederick is happy to be the bait."

Verity gave a short, sharp laugh at this.

"Alphonso already knows him as the vampire slayer, you can be sure. That man will not stir a muscle for Frederick but, oh yes, he will bite him and straight away, before you have even had time to lift your crucifix, Lawrence. If we are talking about risks, Frederick faces a far more grave one were you to use that plan. To me, that is madness."

Lawrence did not say a word and, sensing she was winning him over, Verity steamed ahead.

"Are you saying then that you do not believe you can protect me, or kill Alphonso for that matter, were I to lure him to you?"

155

"No, of course not. We could do both, and I know Frederick has faced far worse in his past."

"Well, then you have as good as approved my plan, Lawrence, and besides, it could be only days until the supreme Master lands, brought in by this evil man, Alphonso. Then all hell will really be let loose and I, and many others, will be in mortal danger! Who would you rather deal with – this foreign man who I can wind round my little finger, or the unknown, shadowy, all-powerful Master?"

Lawrence sighed. He sensed he was losing the battle on every front.

"It will be infinitely harder to battle the Master," he admitted, "But, even were I to agree to your plan, we still have to get round Frederick and he will not be easy."

"So, you do agree to my plan then?"

Lawrence was torn. In one sense he embraced it but…

"It is a terrible risk you are taking, Verity," he said now, "You place your absolute trust in us two and what if we were to fail you?"

"I will bite your necks for eternity for doubting me and my plan," she laughed.

"This is deadly serious," continued Lawrence, obviously troubled.

Silence fell again and the man wrestled with his thoughts, whereas Verity was quietly confident she had won.

"I take this risk freely," she acknowledged, spreading her hands, "Say you will at least talk to Frederick about it. Oh, yes, and promise me one thing."

"Anything, dear lady."

"Do not breathe a word to Liddy," finished Verity and prepared to leave.

Frederick was appalled that Lawrence appeared to have come round to Verity's way of thinking.

"Do you not realise how dangerous this is?" he kept repeating.

156

"It is far more dangerous to let the Master into our village whereby it will not just be Verity's life in danger," replied Lawrence calmly. He suspected his friend of having intense feelings for this woman but nothing had ever been said between them. He felt certain Verity had a deep regard for Frederick but if it was merely gratitude or love he had no way of telling. Nor was it any of his business, he judged. He was far too old for such matters.

"I think Verity knows her own mind," he said now, when Frederick looked certain to explode.

"She does not grasp the gravity of the situation at all," the man replied, shaking his head, "Why, I would rather she face that pack of curs who protect him than that man. Dog bites heal but a bite from a vampire? She is doomed to wander for eternity then."

"Unless you pierce her heart, as you have done to so many others. One thing is sure, you will have no trouble in sending her love," put in Lawrence. He could not resist it.

"What is that supposed to mean?" Frederick almost shouted. He managed to calm himself with difficulty but repeated that Verity was not to be involved under any circumstances.

"How she has pulled you over to her side, I do not know," Frederick continued, a little more calmly.

"Who says she has?" replied his friend, "No other plan asserts itself that will work and time runs out for us."

"You think Verity's plan WILL work?"

"It has a good chance, yes."

"A good chance? If it fails we have yet another vampire in the neighbourhood and the Master will still come to be received by yet another familiar!"

Lawrence regarded his friend closely.

"It is not like you to be so negative," he continued, "Are there any other factors involved here I should know about?" Frederick reacted as though he had been stung.

"I don't know what you are talking about," he professed. Lawrence leaned back in his chair and regarded his friend critically.

157

"Feelings should never be allowed to get in the way of duty. Remember that my friend?"

"Just what are you alluding to, Lawrence?" said his friend, rather sharply, "Come on, spit it out, since you would burden me with another problem as well as Verity's apparent death-wish!"

"Very well then. How shall I put it? Affairs of the heart!"

Frederick got up like he had been shot and turned his face away from his friend.

"The only heart I wish to consider is the staked one of Alphonso, once we have killed him," he said at length.

"So, you will leave without a backward glance when the bloodsuckers are finally destroyed in this area and it is time to go to Scotland or Wales or…?"

"I shall indeed," cut in Frederick, "I have had enough of this grim moorland and its dark secret. I realise what you are alluding to, even though you will not say it straight out. When have you known me to set my cap at a woman, Lawrence?"

"I haven't," came the honest reply.

"Well then, my dear friend, drop the subject entirely before you and I fall out. If you have so much energy, I wish you would put it into devising another plan that does not involve Miss Whittle."

Lawrence smiled but knew his words had hit home, 'Miss Whittle' she might be to Frederick when he was questioned, but there seemed no doubt he thought of her with at least some fondness. Whether that would affect the plan Verity had so laboriously worked out, Lawrence did not know but he sensed he was going to find out.

CHAPTER THIRTEEN

"I still can't believe we are doing this," said Frederick, some three days later, as they watched the sky darken over and an early February dusk descend. Lawrence put out his hand to his friend.
"It will be alright," he murmured, "Verity is word perfect and our practices have gone smoothly."
    Frederick shivered.
"Too smoothly," he said.
"We must not be negative," continued Lawrence, "Confidence will win the day."
"I have a...what is it...a foreboding about this," whispered Frederick, more to himself than anything.
    Lawrence did not reply; he felt as though he was part of someone else's reverie. Instead he repeated success, success, to himself, under his breath. Divine power is on our side, he told himself – the power of Christ who came to save every sinner from the lake of fire and brimstone. Lawrence had faith that this God would protect Verity too.
"Goodness will prevail," he said now, aloud.
    They were waiting for Verity to dress but Frederick was beyond restless and they had elected to wait outside in the end.
"You have everything with you and you have checked and checked?"
"A thousand times, my friend," replied Lawrence.
    The door opened behind them and Verity appeared. Both men gasped, she was a vision of loveliness.
Verity looked from one to the other and asked,
"There! Will I do?"
Frederick felt more uncomfortable than ever.
"You are enough to charm an angel from the upward paths, indeed you are miss!" from Lawrence. Frederick it seemed could not speak.
Verity pulled her veil down and smiled.

It was a couple of hours later and darkness had obliterated every trace of light from the winter sky. The moorland hung, drab and grey, waiting for the first breath of spring to come and banish its long sleep. It seemed winter was frozen in an icy dance but the moorland slept on, knowing that only sunshine and warmth would bring fresh movement to the region. It was in limbo and heavy, heavy did its mood seem that February evening.

Three people walked its rain-soaked pathways and the leader, a tall, well-built man turned to his female companion and said beseechingly,

"It is not too late to change your mind, Verity. What if your uncle is here? Why, he will recognise you and once that happens then the game will be over."

"How come?" replied the woman evenly, "I can keep him away with love as I have every night for the last few weeks or so. However, no such emotion will be sent to Alphonso and the fear I feel about him is real; that will draw him in like a fly to rotting meat! He has only seen me once and the bloodlust will overcome any fear he has for his safety once he sees I am alone."

Frederick felt sick.

"Let me take your place and give me the brooch so I may pierce my skin. My blood will be enough to satisfy him, I am sure, but of course I am far too clever to let him bite me!"

"So am I," returned Verity, defiantly. She removed the brooch from her cloak pocket and drew back her sleeve.

"Don't! Don't!" cried Frederick, and by the dim light of Lawrence's lantern Verity could see tears sparkling in his eyes.

They had nearly reached Alphonso's lair and the dogs were howling. The moon was shrouded in silence and the three of them fell under its spell.

"Are you sure you have everything to hand?" Frederick asked, breaking the heavy stillness of the night air.

"How many times have you done this my friend, and yet, still you feel you need to ask such a question?" Lawrence retorted, "More to the point have I ever failed you?"

160

Frederick did not reply to that.

Verity regarded the candles burning in the windows of the house ahead of them.

"He has not drawn the shutters down as yet," she said simply. True, fear assailed her but, in that terror, there was a measure of defiance for her uncle.

"You will not slaughter the innocent that lay sleeping in their beds around here," she chanted as if to boost her spirits, "Uncle Richard I love, love, love you." She could feel the revulsion such words caused to the Undead and her uncle's disgust came back on the night wind and ruffled her hood. The vibration of love was too high for him, and its purity bit into his flesh. He was close, she was sure of that, but not in the house they now faced. Possibly he was wandering the moorland, searching for prey but he would elude her and his footsteps would follow other paths.

She gazed at the wound and knew Frederick was appalled by what she had done to herself. Lawrence, she knew, was stoic over such an action.

"Blood to end bloodshed," he had said. She tried to reassure Frederick now but he avoided her eye, and that was easy in the darkness.

They drew ever closer. Lawrence folded the shutters on the lantern and now they were in total darkness, apart from the shine of the candles in the windows only a few feet away from them.

"There is still time," began Frederick, having one last try, but Verity shook her hood and touched his cold hand.

"We have waited too long as it is," she cut in, "The Supreme Master could be on his way this very night."

Frederick shivered.

"Let us hope not," he whispered, in a worried tone.

"While the wound leaks so freely, I am off and the rest of this road I must tread alone," Verity continued, "Be vigilant, men, for I shall try and get him to search for my brooch right under your feet as it were, so you may pounce and thus end his reign of terror. Make sure you are well hidden for he will smell you, I fear. I have dropped my handkerchief where the trinket lays and it has the added attraction of my blood on it too." She had reached the stables and she saw they were securely locked and bolted.

"He has brought more boxes in since we were last here," murmured Lawrence but Frederick merely nodded, all of his attention on Verity. She drew off into the darkness.

"Goodbye," she whispered, "When I see you both again Alphonso will have sacrificed his Undead status for the gates of Heaven."

"For the bowels of hell," growled Frederick, "If he so much as touches one hair on her head..."

"He will not," Lawrence reassured him, "We will have him before his plans become reality, never fear, my friend. The fly walks into the web and the spider pounces."

Silence washed over them all and Frederick could no longer see Verity but he knew she must be very near the back door of the dwelling. His legs felt like jelly but even so he longed to run after her and take her place in this dangerous charade. Yet, if he did and put a hand on her shoulder, she would shake him off like gossamer and continue on her way into the jaws of Hell.

Verity had reached her target and, although her heart beat wildly, she rapped loudly upon the door.

"Help me, please!" she cried, knowing her voice would reach the men waiting in the wings of the scene as it were. The wound was now bleeding profusely and she felt the occasional drop falling on her feet as she stood silent, overcome by the gravity of the situation she was facing. "Help!" she cried again, even louder.

Suddenly the light moved from the window and the barking of dogs was hushed, although one or two continued to howl but from what seemed like further away. Alphonso must have shut them up, she concluded. Hurried footsteps from behind the door confirmed the man was coming, unless he had a servant he had summoned. Verity was excited, terrified and enthralled all at once. The bolts drew back and Verity was face to face with those cold, blue eyes that sent a chill into the very core of her being. She thrust her injured

162

hand forward and she saw Alphonso's expression change from one of anger to extreme torment.

Blood...fresh blood.

She could see his hands shaking by the way the candle moved in them and he turned away from the door, as if to try and control himself. She had already seen those things that terrified her; the shine of a wolf in his eyes and the snarl of a bear in the expression of his mouth. Those teeth! If she failed to play this to the letter, those huge canines would be piercing her skin and impaling her on the branch of eternity. She shuddered.

"What has happened?" he said, keeping his face averted from hers and from the wound still dripping blood on his doorstep. She saw him pierce his own skin with his nails, so strong was the blood lust and she knew she had him trapped and cornered. She pressed on.

"Oh, Mr Darling! I have injured myself on the moor and cannot stop the blood from flowing and I have lost a most valuable heirloom. Whilst I have been searching for it the light has left the sky and now it wants..."

"But a few moments to the witching hour, madam, I assure you," he flung back at her.

"Indeed. Please can you help me?" She tried to make the latter sentence as soft and alluring as she could and, pressing home her advantage, she lightly touched the shoulder that was turned to her. Alphonso winced.

"You are out very late!" he snarled, "You must go home. It is...not very safe here."

"But how can I leave, Mr Darling," she wheedled, "Without my prize possession?" and she touched his arm once more. He reacted as though he had been burnt and the candle leapt from his hand and extinguished itself on the hall mat. Alphonso scuffed it off, cursing loudly.

"Are you alone then?" he asked, regarding her now that the darkness was on his side.

"Quite," she reassured him.

A hint of a smile crossed his lips but Verity saw nothing, standing now with no light to see his movements and feeling very vulnerable. If he leapt upon her now…

He drew off a little and murmured that he would fetch a lantern as the candle was spent, then they would go.

The wind rose and blew upon Verity as she waited, as calmly as she could, for the man to prepare himself. He returned presently with a cloak and hat on, a slatted lantern in his hand.

"What, may I ask, Miss Whittle, have you lost?" he enquired.

"A priceless brooch, Mr Darling. It was left to me by my father and it was his mother's I believe. Gold, jewels and mother of pearl grace its face but alas, it is lost in the heather!"

"You know where?"

"I dropped my white handkerchief to mark the spot and, as long as the wind has not blown it away, we will find it I am sure!"

He turned to her and his eyes flashed fire.

"You have every faith in me it seems, Miss Whittle," he sneered, and she saw the shine of his teeth and his wet mouth in a moonbeam that lit the path they trod. He left his outer door open as though he meant to return very soon and Verity shuddered. With her as insensible prey, she surmised.

"We will find the trinket," he said now, when he saw she had stopped.

"It is no trinket I assure you, Mr Darling. Why, it is worth thousands!"

"Is it indeed?" he returned calmly, "Well, let us go on. When we have the treasure safe, then you can return to mine and let me dress your wound. You will find I have a way with injuries…a healing hand many would say as, after my intervention, the infirmity will trouble you no more," He turned to her again and raised the lantern.

"See how the cut bleeds in the cold!" he almost shouted, as he saw the glint of blood on her sleeve. He controlled himself with difficulty and asked her if she could cover it for now, until he had time to attend to it.

"My handkerchief is gone, sir, and I do not possess another!" she replied, moving forward once more. He passed her one of his gloves but she saw his hands were shaking and he was biting his lips with some force.

Blood...fresh blood, sang his heart and soul.

The handkerchief showed up like a white dove in a sea of darkness and Alphonso fell upon it and pressed it to his lips. Blood, dried it is true but lately shed and with that metallic taste that drove him wild for more. More, of course, was standing right beside him, pints of it flowing in her warm, virginal veins. He almost swooned. His lips sucked the dried essence and his attention was completely on satisfying the uncontrollable urge such a smell occasioned, so he did not see the two figures creeping up to him. Suddenly, with a huge blow, Frederick struck…

The vampire was quite overcome with surprise and for a moment he was overpowered. Lawrence began sprinkling Holy Water over his face and Alphonso screamed aloud in agony.

How it burns! How it burns! Yet his mind was recovering and with it his strength. He flung the handkerchief from him and writhed this way and that.

"In the name of Christ and all the saints of Heaven, surrender your eternal life of sin and give up your black soul to God!" Lawrence shouted, pressing the crucifix into the man's face. His flesh sizzled like he was on fire and Alphonso writhed even more, mad with pain.

He began kicking out with his legs and Frederick found he was in danger of losing hold of the man. Lawrence jumped to weigh down the vampire's legs, which were inflicting massive blows to his friend. Between the two of them they were able to subdue the man once more, but all question of one of them raising the stake was impossible.

"Hold him! Hold him!" yelled Frederick, when he felt the vampire's strength returning, "Verity, grab the tools and come closer!"

Verity did as she was told, for the tools were now scattered in the heather but with the use of Alphonso's lantern she located them and stood ready. However, both Lawrence and Frederick had underestimated the man's power and it was growing increasingly difficult to keep him on the ground. All the time those sharp white teeth, with just a tint of Verity's dried blood upon them, were gnashing ever closer to Frederick's face.

The vampire hunters redoubled their efforts and Frederick ground his knees into the man's chest, whilst Lawrence tried to deal with the flailing legs.

"Mercy! Mercy!" yelled Alphonso, "I am not who you think I am but the Master will come and destroy you all, including that bitch who stands so close and threatens me!"

"Mind your manners in front of a lady!" returned Frederick, infuriated by the vampire's words.

To Verity he cried,

"You have to strike whilst we have him contained. If he gets away we are all done for!"

Verity looked at the stake and mallet in her hands with horror.

"I...I...cannot," she sobbed.

Alphonso saw she hesitated and tried to press home an advantage.

"Come to me! Come to me!" he called. "We will make sweet music for eternity! Another thirty years and these mortals will be in the grave!"

"Do it! Do it!" screamed Lawrence, losing hold of the man briefly as the vampire's strength increased, "His teeth are near Frederick's face, Verity, and it only takes one bite...one bite!"

"Verity! In God's name help us!" pleaded Frederick, as a huge tongue tried to lick him and he smelt the overpowering stench of fetid breath. "Verity….I love you so much. Please save me! Save me! We cannot hold him much longer and he will bite me first!"

The words washed over Verity but the sheer horror of the situation meant she could not dwell on them.

"I love you Alphonso...I love you," cried Verity, noticing how her words subdued the man and took his strength away. "God loves you too and all the saints in Heaven and Jesus Christ as well! He died for you and He will wash your sin away till your black soul is as white as the clouds of Paradise. St Peter waits for you at the gate and he turns the key. Bless you, Alphonso, bless you," and she tipped the remaining Holy Water over the man's upturned face.

The vampire cried aloud for mercy but Verity pressed on. "We all love you here. We all love you. Depart now, with a blessing on your lips, and receive God's Holy love."

The vampire was cursing but his power was not yet diminished and he gave one massive surge to try and bite Frederick. Verity saw she had no choice but to strike and, raising the stake and mallet, she stepped forward and hit true.

"I love you Alphonso, I love you Alphonso, love..." chanted all three and then, suddenly, only silence was left to dwell in the stagnant darkness of the moorland. With one huge cry of surrender, Alphonso gave up his life and was still. It was over.

CHAPTER FOURTEEN

It seemed darker than ever on the moors after Alphonso died. Frederick moved to comfort Verity as she stood, in a trance, with only her raiment moving in the night wind. He looked deep into her eyes and tried to convince her everything was going to be alright.

"The Master cannot come now," he whispered, "We will smash up the coffins and scatter the earth to the four winds, far and wide, so as to confuse him."

Verity turned her beautiful but sad eyes upon him.

"There is my uncle," she sobbed, "My flesh and blood. Alphonso was nothing but the greatest challenge, at least for me, is yet to come."

It was three days later. Frederick and Lawrence, true to their word, had reduced the coffins to firewood, burning them with a prayer, and had ridden for miles to throw handfuls of earth into the air and thus thwart the Master's coming. His native soil now lay in clumps over two counties and he had no base to call home. Besides, Alphonso was dead and any operations he had been planning were definitely postponed.

Verity had recovered and felt somewhat more stoical as to what had to be done to lay her uncle to rest.

"I have felt his sufferings in my dreams," she said, "Always my love enfolds him so he cannot hurt me but it burns him with the fire of purity and he wails and gnashes his teeth in agony. There is only one way he can ever be at peace. When the land is covered with darkness he is forced to wander, driven on by the blood lust that has taken over his soul. How can he be happy? Does he even know what happiness is? Only the stake can bring him the eternal bliss he seeks."

The man had been seen ripping out sheep's throats to drink their blood and end, if temporarily, the soul-wrenching lust he felt. However, on the next night, the moon would rise again and he would be forced to wander, seeking yet more nourishment. Luckily, so far, no further humans had fallen prey to his teeth.

"We must act soon," Frederick told Verity, fearing for her sanity but knowing time was short.

Verity nodded. She had been very quiet since Alphonso had been destroyed and any words she had uttered had fallen upon Jet's black, sensitive ears. To both Liddy and Frederick, she seemed like a closed book.

"Are you ready, Verity, for I believe your uncle wanders around Alphonso's old dwelling searching for company when the wind is at its loneliest? Yet again, it may take two of us to subdue the man. Look at Alphonso..." Frederick reminded her.

Verity shivered and buried her head in Jet's glossy, black fur.

"I am ready," she said, at length.

Her silences were partly due to her mind, reminding her constantly that she was a murderess, but she told herself a hundred times a day that Alphonso was not a man but a ghoul, a vampire, a bloodsucker. Furthermore, the choice was to kill the ringleader or to let Frederick join him to greet the Master. No matter how many times she told herself that, it always came back to the fact that by her hands, and her hands alone, the creature had died.

To save Frederick, she whispered.

She turned her hands over fifty or more times every day and looked at the pale pink palms. Should they not be stained with blood for eternity, she wondered, and the fires of Hell seemed very near during those dark hours.

"A man died because of you," she told her reflection, over and over again. Yet the dark shadows under her eyes and the wan skin, seemed punishment enough for killing a vampire. May St Peter open the gates of Heaven to Alphonso, she prayed night after night.

Even so another, darker force drew nearer and threatened to destroy her world...

169

After the last two vampires were killed Frederick would be leaving. She remembered his words uttered in sheer panic as Alphonso's teeth loomed ever nearer.

"Verity! I love you! Save me! "

They haunted her at night when sleep escaped her and her wandering imagination conjured up bats, bats, bats, filling the wall outside her bedroom. Yet with Alphonso's death the bats had been scattered and not so much as the snap of bony wings echoed in the night sky.

"I love you! I love you!" screamed Frederick, but the words seemed to mock her and she believed he had only said them in order to save his life.

Not true, not true, said another, saner part of her mind. Frederick is a loyal and honest man.

Nothing more had been said between them since that night but Verity knew he regarded her as frail and the part she had to play in destroying her uncle weighed heavily on the vampire hunter's mind. If he could do it alone, without including her, she knew he would but her heart did not feel it was fair to expect this. Surely this ghastly nightmare was something of her own making, as Richard was her relation? She understood why the eyes of the village were upon her when she ventured abroad and she saw distrust and fear there too.

Her own feelings for Frederick were as clear as day; she loved the man but how could she encourage such an emotion when his path lay so far away from her?

Whilst Verity was recovering, Lawrence and Frederick sought Rose's friend, who had escaped on bony, sinewy wings that night when they tempted them with blood.

"Fancy was supposed to be holed up in Cliffe's Wood," Frederick remembered, "However, that was days ago and she may have moved on by now."

"It is a starting point, nevertheless," replied Lawrence, checking he had all the equipment they needed for a long night vampire hunting.

"She may already have stripped the trees of life and gone elsewhere to smell out fresh blood," his friend came back with. He seemed very absent-minded and Lawrence had not seen him like this before but the night ahead of them was going to be difficult enough without raising fresh problems to mull over, so Lawrence stayed quiet. He knew there would always be mortals who were attracted to the idea of eternal life, even if that life meant being torn apart by the blood lust, and so the last two vampires could easily become ten or more if humans crossed their paths.

The woods were very overgrown and Frederick and Lawrence tripped over brambles and the remnants of hundreds of years of decay. Ivy strangled the screaming trees, strange, malevolent fungi grew in every crack and crevice and, at this time of the year, the place presented a sorry face.

Dusk was coming down resolutely and both Frederick and Lawrence carried lanterns as the floor of the wood was strewn with large pieces of rock too.

"This is more dangerous than what we face with the vampires, dear friend," murmured Lawrence, as he stumbled for the sixth time. Frederick jerked his attention back to the tangled paths but did not speak.

They pressed on. Stopping in a slight clearance Lawrence asked his companion if he heard anything.

"No," replied Frederick, "The silence deafens me to be honest."

"You seem troubled..." began Lawrence.

"It is facing Richard, Verity's uncle, that perturbs me," came the answer.

"And Verity herself?"

Frederick was suspicious.

"What do you mean?" he asked guardedly.

"What you said...I mean, I know your life was in danger but..." Lawrence knew he was on very dangerous ground and he waited for the outburst but it never came.

"I meant every word," said Frederick at length, in a sad voice.

They were prevented from further dialogue by a loud noise to their left and the flapping of bony wings, above the prison of trees, reached their ears.

"It's her!" yelled Lawrence and bloodshot eyes were turned upon him, "Quick! She remembers us and seeks to escape!"

The vampire turned her fury upon them.

"YOU!" she screeched, "You tempted us with blood – foul, stale blood, and you killed my friend, our sister, Rose!"

"She was Undead and thus tormented so we released her soul to the best eternal life there is, one that exists beyond the gates of Heaven with God!"

Fancy screamed at the mention of God and Lawrence leapt and pressed the cross to her leg so her height was diminished and she fell on to the ground beneath their feet. A loud hissing sound ensued and Fancy writhed in pain. Seeking to escape, she stretched her wings but Frederick was ready for her and a huge cascade of Holy Water drained her power.

Screeching like a banshee, she rolled over in the leaf mast and Lawrence pinned her down at once.

"Open your heart – your damned, black heart and receive the love of Christ," he yelled at her, "Receive God's Holy love and be surrounded by it. May your soul turn from the darkness and seek the paths of light!" he chanted at her, throwing more Holy Water over her face. Flailing desperately and almost blinded by the water she sent clouds of beech mast over the two men but Frederick had immobilised her with his weight and turned her round so that Lawrence could strike. She snapped at him like a harpy but he managed to evade her teeth and Lawrence raised the stake and took up the mallet, praying as he did so,

"O Lord, forgive me for what I am about to do. Fancy – may true love be yours, may peace and mercy be yours, may eternal life in God's kingdom be yours. Surrender your soul to Christ!" He struck clean and after one strangled cry from her impaled body, silence came and washed over them. Suddenly, as they watched, the shrieking vampire with its bloodshot eyes and curled talons vanished from their view and a young, beautiful girl emerged looking as though she had just gone to sleep.

"That was almost too easy for my liking," murmured Frederick, climbing to his feet, "It resonates as a bad omen."

Lawrence dusted his clothes down and turned to look at the sweetly smiling girl.

"Be grateful for small mercies, my friend," was all he said.

They buried Fancy in the end in the wooded glade.

"We cannot face the inquisition and the fury that was unleashed over Rose's death," Frederick said, throwing to one side the piece of trunk they had used as a spade. "I know it seems wrong but we have interred her and we said a prayer as she expired."

Lawrence mentioned that it might be worth keeping this night's work from Verity for fear of upsetting her.

"Look how devastated she was over Rose and she nearly broke down and revealed all..."

"She did not!" flashed Frederick, but he calmed then and mentioned that Verity had already asked about Fancy and even remembered the haunt of this lady.

"She asked me only yesterday what we planned to do about it," he finished.

"So, did you enlighten her?" asked Lawrence, corking the empty water bottle and wiping the stake on the leafy ground.

"Verity and I do not have any secrets from each other," Frederick told him.

"I can believe that," Lawrence admitted, "Seeing as you opened your heart to her last week. I trust you received a satisfactory answer back to your declaration?"

Frederick laughed.

"Oh yes," he sneered, "It is just the time to swear undying love to your friend, as you drive a stake through a vampire's heart!"

"But you have been together since?" continued Lawrence, surprised to find his companion so willing to expound on the subject.

"Do you really think Verity can come to terms with what she did, in just a few, short days?" asked Frederick, as they left Cliffe's Wood.

Lawrence shrugged.

"Affairs of the heart have never been my speciality," he admitted, "So, where do you stand now on leaving, since you have such powerful feelings for the lady and there is every chance she may return them?"

Frederick stopped. He was exhausted and there was still Verity's uncle to face. Lawrence turned to him and tugged at his sleeve.

"We may have extinguished Satan's light here," he said gently, "But messengers come daily to tell me of other vampire lairs in other counties and what do I tell them?"

Frederick sighed and gazed up at the firmament with its sparkling silver set of stars.

"You tell them we will attend to those devils when we finish here," he replied, and then would not be drawn on the subject any more that night.

The next day at noon, Frederick rose and went to see Verity. He needed to know if she was strong enough to face her uncle in the final showdown any time soon. Reports suggested the vampire was frequenting the empty stables at Alphonso's every night, clearly waiting for the ultimate Master to arrive and save him. His wails were quite loud enough for most of the village to hear and, even worse, he had chased after a small boy, tending to sheep at five o'clock in the morning on one of the outlying farms around Alphonso's dwelling. Luckily, the youngster had got away. Frederick shivered. One bite and the whole sordid scene would start again.

He found Verity grooming Jet and feeding him minced morsels of raw mutton. At first he felt loath to even mention the subject he had come about, as the cat and the woman seemed in such complete harmony. But after Jet had demolished a plateful and had sunk to sleep on Verity's lap, he began cautiously,

"You know Lawrence and I will try to subdue your uncle if you still feel the task of helping us is beyond you."

Verity jumped at his words and the warmth and comfort of her world crashed about her ears.

"Have I ever said I would leave you to face that danger alone?" she asked.

"No," began Frederick, feeling he had blundered in too fast as usual, "What you did concerning Alphonso could have been done by no other woman I know."

"Do you have many female acquaintances then, Frederick?" The man blushed a little at this.

"No," he said again, wondering how Verity managed to turn the attention back on himself so swiftly.

"I mean there was my mother and two sisters and they would all have run a mile!"

"Ah! So, you think I am made of sterner stuff then!"

"Don't tease me, Verity. You know as well as I do what I think of you, but we have this last, massive problem in the form of..."

"My uncle and thus, my responsibility."

"No, not at all. However, your help in calling the man forth would be very much appreciated. He will come for you, as you are his flesh and blood."

Verity shivered.

"I wish I was not," she said, "Tell me how you mean to apprehend him and I will aid you."

Frederick drained his cup and Verity moved to refill it, disturbing Jet who walked off in disdain and sought a far chair to finish his nap upon.

"Ah, Frederick, your thirst has upset my companion and thrown him out of his blissful sleep!"

Frederick smiled and was grateful for the mirth to lift the mood, for a sombre silence seemed to have gathered in the room.

"Apologies to Jet, I am sure...Our plan is this, Verity. Your uncle seems to be frequenting Alphonso's house, night after night with regularity..."

"Ah – I suppose the gypsies told you that?"

"No, they have gone," Frederick told her, "But a friend of Lawrence's, eager to earn himself a shilling, has been staking out the place."

"An unfortunate turn of phrase there, Frederick, staking, and one that Alphonso would find far from funny concerning his house!"

Frederick grinned. Really, Verity was in a lively mood today and almost back to her usual self.

"It will not be his house for much longer, as I understand from Mrs Binns that his rent was only paid up to the end of the month."

"Time passes so quickly, Frederick, and as one month comes in another speeds past us and goes out."

"Indeed," Frederick was slightly nettled at her constant interruptions.

"Anyway, both Lawrence and I will go tonight to check that he does indeed wander that way and then, when you feel ready, you can accompany us to try and draw him out of the shadows."

"You do not need me tonight then?"

"No, and if I had my way we would try to manage alone but the blood tie between you and he is what could bring us victory. How do you feel, Verity, about your last relation being staked and despatched in that way? You said on the moorland, after Alphonso had been killed, that your greatest trial was to come with Richard. Do you still feel that is so?"

Verity sighed and took a moment or two to answer. Frederick tried to be patient but he was clearly on tenterhooks for her reply.

"I have had plenty of time to mull this over," she said at length, "And the man was dead before I came here, so how can I mourn his demise now, when I feel his torment every night?"

"Does he still come to you in dreams then?"

"Yes, frequently, but the love vibration stalls him and I know that will be the final means of placing him within reach of heaven. Whether St Peter will open the gate to any of these black scoundrels I do not know but I feel there is hope of reconciling him to God. My parents would have wanted it, had they known what had occurred here."

Frederick let out a long sigh of relief. He was hoping to get away without mentioning Fancy when Verity suddenly asked him.

"What of the other girl you were taking care of? Where is she? Still in Cliffe's Wood?"

"Yes," replied Frederick, and felt his answer was at least an honest one.

However Verity was not to be fooled.

"Alive or dead?" she continued, "Or rather Undead or dead, I should have said."

"I prefer to say she is at peace," Frederick told her and stood up to leave.

"So you buried her there, did you, instead of bringing her back to the village? Is there a family looking for her?"

"She had no family, Verity, and we said a prayer over her."

"But no flowers...no compassion. I bet she turned back into a beautiful child once the curse was lifted from her."

Frederick had to admit she did but he maintained that she would not be missed and no family waited anxiously for news of her.

"So, you are happy for the worms to gobble her up?"

"Happy would not be the word I would choose to use but we needed to inter her in case questions were asked."

Verity could see the sense of that and the two parted with Frederick promising to come on the morrow and inform her of what occurred at Reeve's End. The owner would take the mansion back very soon and they needed to act quickly before Richard picked the man off as vampire fodder.

However, neither had said what was uppermost in their hearts. Verity knew, once Richard was dead, Frederick would go and she would never see him again.

CHAPTER FIFTEEN

March was almost here and the grateful moorland sent out gnarled hands to the verdant spring that was surely just around the corner. No longer was it dark by five o'clock in the evenings and the mornings were lighter too, although the cold persisted.

Frederick and Lawrence decided to visit Reeve's End about midnight, when they hoped Richard would be at his most verbal, and they could then get a clear idea of how difficult it would be to entrap the man.

"Alphonso's tenancy ends in eleven days according to Mrs Binns," Frederick said, as they made their way through the dried heather to the mansion, "What will the owner make of his property after this strange period of time, I wonder?"

"He is in grave danger of becoming fodder for Richard, if we do not do anything," replied Lawrence.

"Exactly, my dear friend. Thus, I have brought everything we need, just in case the vampire decides to surrender his life to us tonight, and then Verity will not be needed."

Lawrence smiled into the silent darkness. There was not much moonlight and the wind was piercingly cold.

"I presume you saw her today and do not want to trouble her if we can help it?" he asked.

"Accurate as always," admitted Frederick, "She joked and laughed with me but her eyes were distant and so was her heart."

"What about your heart, my friend?"

Frederick sighed.

"It remains the same, as strong as when I declared my love on the moors, the day Alphonso died," he replied, "If anything, with the imminent departure, my feelings are sharper, clearer but she has said nothing to me, although I hinted that my words, spoken then, were true."

"So you still mean to go when Richard is at Abraham's bosom?"

"If Verity says nothing...yes."

They strode on in silence and Reeve's End was soon reached. It was dark and foreboding and, looking in, they could see a half-spent candle leaning drunkenly against the pane. When they had returned to smash up the coffins, Frederick, who like Verity adored animals, had released the dogs and sent them on over the moorlands where at least they had a chance of freedom and life. Luckily, so great was their desire to escape, they had not noticed him and had sped off, presumably looking for their master. Alphonso had been buried, very quickly, near a lime pit on the moors.

The house emitted a peculiar silence and after a quick survey of the property the men took up a post near the old stables where the coffins had been stored. They did not have to wait long before footsteps on the gravel announced the arrival of a visitor.

"Alphonso! Alphonso! Where are you?" yelled the man, who they realised must be Richard. He sounded bereft and was sobbing between words. "Why, oh why, do you evade me and where is the Ultimate Master who you said would come to save us all? Alphonso - answer me! Where have you gone? Not even a dog barking or the light of a candle in the window. I cannot take this loneliness! Not a soul to talk to and Fancy lies cold and dead in Cliffe's Wood. Yes, I drained her body of blood but much good has it done me! Alphonso! Alphonso! Why have you left me?"

"The man is clearly disturbed and, as such, not thinking straight, so it should be easy to overpower him," whispered Frederick, "Then we do not need to trouble Verity at all. She said Alphonso's death was nothing to this one and Richard is, after all, her only flesh and blood. She told me she had come to terms with it but I heard the hesitancy in her voice and I fear for her sanity. Should we ask her to take an active part in her own uncle's demise?"

Lawrence was not so sure.

"I think you underestimate her," he murmured back, "I believe she is strong enough to deal with this. We do not want the man to escape but tonight was for watching and assessing..."

179

"Can't you hear the fear in his voice? He will be easy for us to kill, thus we can tell Verity her nightmares are over!"
"He still haunts her sleep then I take it?"
"Yes. However, she keeps him away with the love vibration."
"Exactly. She is strong, Frederick, and as such, she will want to be there when we send Richard to meet his maker."
"I disagree, my friend. We should strike now, whilst he is lost in sorrow and distress."

Richard began to search the empty outbuildings, bewailing his solitary state and calling aloud for deliverance from this abandonment.
"There you are," whispered Frederick, "He is easy prey for the two of us. Have you the tools I asked you to bring?"
Lawrence admitted he had.
"Bring them forth and stand ready then, for when he enters this stable I shall grab him and hold him down, whilst you despatch him with a blessing."

Lawrence still disapproved of the plan but was willing to go along with it, seeing Frederick was so assured. They waited until the ring of the vampire's footsteps sounded outside the stable, and the door was opened, and then, rallying forth, Frederick attempted to apprehend the man with the element of surprise.

True, Richard was immersed in grief but his reactions were still fast and self preservation was always on his mind. He not only saw but he felt Frederick's hands come out to grab him and he jumped back.
"Ah...the vampire slayer and somewhere his sidekick!" yelled the creature, now out of reach of Frederick's grasp.
"Murderers, the two of you! Mass murderers and you have kept my niece from me too! I abhor the love she tried to send me! Ah...I nearly had her once before your meddling and you have clearly murdered Alphonso too and scattered the Master's precious life soil I know not where!"
"They are gone to the four corners of the earth," shouted Lawrence, "You alone in this region remain as Undead. A forlorn and unhappy future awaits you! Surrender your life

to us now and Jesus will extend love and forgiveness to you surely!"

At the mention of Jesus and love the vampire set up a furious howling.

"Love?" he cried, "A twisted, bitter emotion that threatens to take my eternal life from me! Why, the maidens at my party promised me everlasting life and I took it with just a bite. I wanted my niece to join me...family, at last, you might say, but you thwarted me at every turn. I will have my family. I WILL!" He turned furious, blood red eyes on the two men and, suddenly, with a bony snap of wings, he was skyward, out of the stables and vanishing into the dark night air.

Frederick raced out of the building, throwing Holy Water into the ether but it only came back to wet him and the sky was suddenly cold and empty. Richard had gone.

Verity could not sleep. She rose after midnight and, lighting a candle, went down to the parlour where so much of her uncle remained. She started looking through his books and came upon an old diary embossed with a date, some twenty years back, which he had evidently used recently, till just before his death. Turning the pages brought some interest, as she read the accounts of growing crops and the harvesting of fruit and vegetables but then a new theme took hold and made her eyes light up.

"I am seemingly forced out of my solitude by fair maidens," Richard wrote, "For one turned up here, lost and lonely, and expressing such an interest in my garden that my desire for seclusion was quite broken. She enthralled me with her beauty and has promised to come on the morrow, in order to show me the best way to yield more wheat for my bread. Strangely, she seeks to impart her secret at night, when the moon is high in the sky, so it will be tomorrow, for she maintains that moonlight and magic are what sweeten the rye and plump up the grain and I am anxious to know more."

The next page was torn and what looked like bloodstains remained on the corner but then a highly excited entry for two days later from her uncle:

"How can she do these things to me with a single bite? Not just her either, for there were two of them but, heaven forgive me, my wife is long dead and I have been alone I know not how long. The wound it seems is not keen on healing and she evokes such dreams in me. It is the pathway to eternal life she told me..."

A soft, somewhat hesitant knock at the window. Verity shot bolt upright and dropped the book as though she had been caught snooping. Was it Frederick? Or Lawrence? Could something have happened out there, at Reeve's End, that needed her attention?

"Who is it?" she whispered, anxious not to disturb Liddy. Jet was upstairs, asleep on her bed.

"A man from the village, sent posthaste from the vampire slayer, to say he requires your help with that devil, Richard. I've run all the way in this cold, so could I come in and warm myself for a minute?"

Verity was horrified. She did not recognise the voice but, of course, she did not wander about much in the village. Clearly Frederick or Lawrence were in danger and had sent this man to escort her to them.

"Wait, and I'll open the door for you!" she replied, rushing to the kitchen to find the key. Her mind was on the man she loved and she had forgotten his words from weeks ago, it was true, but they were vital now to her survival.

"Do not let anyone but me, or Lawrence, in after darkness has fallen." It was nearly one o'clock in the morning and never in Verity's life had it been so dark.

Lawrence and Frederick watched the skies for a minute but there was no movement and, even when the moon sailed from a wedge of dark cloud, the heavens were empty.

"We have lost him!" cried Frederick, in exasperation.

"He will know now that we frequent this place at night, so he will come no more," replied Lawrence, "We should have watched and waited, Frederick, like we usually do. When, in the past, have we blundered in with two left feet and sacrificed the day?"

Frederick hung his head. He knew his desire to protect Verity had cost them the trophy. It was the first time his heart had ruled his head and he did not like it but, worse still, that creature would be more elusive than ever to catch.

"He could strike tonight and then we have more to kill," Lawrence murmured. He was very angry but was trying not to show it.

"So where will he go now but to seek prey?" Frederick mused, "Hopefully a sheep on the moor but maybe the village will have left a door or window ajar..."

"He must be invited in first," Lawrence reminded him, "Just as clearly as Verity's uncle invited the maidens in, and thus they bit him, and perpetrated the species. No one in Scar's End will invite a stranger into their dwelling. There are no newcomers, apart from Verity, and the rest know too well what happens if they do. Why, doors and windows are sealed once dusk descends and few venture abroad. Those that do often protect themselves with Holy Water and garlic."

"What of the gypsy camp?" asked Frederick, "Richard pounced on two innocent boys there and don't forget that lad, who saw the creature with red eyes coming after him not a week ago."

"He got away," Lawrence reminded him, "He will not be let out alone when there is a vestige of darkness in the skies. People here take thick sticks to drive the devils off. They are primed now in the folklore of the vampire, for it is on their own doorstep and cannot be ignored."

Frederick felt somewhat comforted by this and turned to the empty building behind them.

"There is no point in remaining any longer," he said, "The bird has flown and quite literally. Richard will not frequent this place any more. Come, let us return home to bed and then meet tomorrow to think this through and ask Verity for her help. For the creature seeks company of his own flesh and blood, and that is her, and her alone."

He did not think what he was saying, so tired and numb was his brain and they gathered up their tools and set off back to the village.

183

Verity rushed to the door, armed with the key, and succeeded in opening it at the second attempt, for the bolts were stiff and needed oiling.

A job for Liddy, she thought, as she pushed the great barrier ajar.

"Are you there?" she called, as loudly as she dared. Liddy slept heavily, she remembered gratefully.

"Yes," came the reply but still the man hesitated on the doorstep and she heard the ring of his boots on stone.

"Come in! Come in!" she cried, "Warm yourself by the dregs of my fire and then we must set off for Reeve's End, where I believe both Lawrence and Frederick are."

The man stepped inside with a nod of his head. He wore a long, dark cloak and his head was covered with the hood.

"You are quite correct," he said, in a clipped tone, "I shall be glad to take shelter for a moment or two and then, as you say, we will be off. You must dress up warmly, as it is a cold night and the wind, particularly, is chill."

Verity noticed he spoke in rather too refined a way for the village men and she wondered who he was but fear that Frederick could be injured, or even dead, put that thought out of her mind.

"Warm your hands by the embers of the fire," she told him, stirring the glowing coals to bring them back to life, "Will you not let down your hood, so I can see you better and you can receive more heat before we go back out there?"

The tall figure laughed.

"I rather think you would change your opinion of me, were I to let down my hood," the visitor said.

Verity was puzzled.

"Who are you then?" she asked, in suspicious tones.

"I think the question should be, who was I?"

Verity began to feel afraid.

"But since you invited me in so freely and this was my house anyway, I will do your bidding," he continued and threw back his dark hood to reveal his face.

Verity was still none the wiser, having not seen her uncle since a small girl. True, he came to her in nightmares but his face was always in shadow.

"You look much older than you sound," she faltered.

"Ah…that is because I am now immortal and, although I may appear to age, my soul is eternally young."

Realisation suddenly dawned on Verity who she faced. "Uncle Richard!" she almost screamed, "What have you done with Frederick and Lawrence?" Forgetting what he was, she ran to him and beat her fists on his head but he threw her off easily.

"Ah, dear niece," he continued, "You talk of ME hurting THEM but who, I ask, is the stake for and why do they seek to burn me with Holy Water and this despicable emotion 'LOVE'?" He spat the word out as though it was choking him and suddenly, Verity remembered her dream.

"I love, love, love you, Uncle Richard!" she screamed as loud as she could, hoping for once Liddy would wake and come to her rescue. She knew Jet was shut in her bedroom and for that she was grateful.

The vampire winced in pain but threw the emotion off as best he could.

"They have murdered all the other vampires in this area and I am alone and bereft," he sobbed, "I want my family round me and you shall join me in the reign of the Undead."

"Never!" declared Verity, picking up the poker to defend herself, "Never."

Upstairs, Jet was far from the land of sleep. He was running round the chamber uttering little cries of despair. He knew, as cats do with their wonderful sixth sense, that his mistress was in danger.

"Let me out! Let me out to save her!" said his plaintive cries, but to the world he let out a series of mews, interspaced with angry hisses.

It was his racing paws that first awakened Liddy and she lay there listening to them, very confused as to what was happening. She got up, found a shawl and some slippers and

185

then let herself out of her room quietly. She could hear Jet crying but she knew from his anxiety and the echo of voices below her, Verity was not in her room.

Judging by the noise from downstairs, Mistress is not alone either, thought Liddy, as the deep tones of a man's voice reached her ears. She listened at the head of the stairs, her hands on the bannisters. Liddy was an excellent eavesdropper and her hearing was sharp and acute. She was grateful for that now, as she could hear every word below and it was obvious to her Verity was in some danger.

"Uncle Richard, I will never, ever go to the shores of eternity with you," Liddy heard her mistress say.

Oh my God she thought, the vampire has found his way to this house…

"This was all mine before the maiden bit me and it will be all mine again when you join me in tasting the euphoria of being Undead," Liddy heard him say, "Do you really think I am leaving, without my only blood relation? Blood! Yes! The heady smell of it quite makes me swoon, and I am hungry for the first bite!"

"I love you, love you, love you, Uncle Richard," she heard Verity repeating, over and over again and then the groans from the vampire as he struggled to approach her.

"I have the purity of love on my side," cried Verity, triumphantly.

Where was Frederick then, wondered Liddy, and should she leave the house and go to find him or would she return, not to one vampire but two?

Verity meanwhile had backed herself into a corner by the bookcase but she remembered putting a Bible in one of the drawers there, only a day or so ago, and now she opened the drawer and snatched it out, thrusting it in her uncle's face.

"Receive the love of Christ from his Holy Book," she shouted, wondering if Liddy was awake as yet.

The book made contact with the vampire's cheek, so close was he, and his flesh sizzled. Verity felt the sickness of revulsion creeping over her but she battled bravely on.

"This book is full of the love of God, which passes all understanding and surrounds you now, Uncle Richard. Do not fight it. Let the pink mist of love creep up on you and trail itself around your heart, around your soul. Our Father who art in Heaven..." she began, praying desperately as she spoke, that Liddy would understand what had happened and would go for help.

But help from whom, if Lawrence and Frederick were at Reeve's End, some half an hour's walk away?

"Give us this day our daily bread and forgive us our trespasses…..see Uncle Richard LOVE, God's love, will set you free..."

It was very dark on the walk back to the village and the moon hid, as though she was afraid to come out of the clouds and face the world. As he walked, Frederick felt very troubled.

This is not right, his heart said. This is not right, said his head.

They breasted a steep hill and suddenly, the village appeared below them, swathed in mist, with here and there the shine of a candle in an open window. It was then two o'clock.

Frederick received a massive jolt in his soul and he knew in an instant where Richard had gone.

"Verity!" he screamed, "Verity! Richard has gone to his kin, his only living relation! Yes, he has gone to bite Verity!" He broke into a run and Lawrence followed suit.

"She will not let him in!" affirmed his friend.

"What if he turns himself into a bat, a cat, Liddy even - all of which he is more than capable of doing? What if he says he brings a message from us? Verity will let him in then, I am sure!"

"But you told her never to open the door after darkness has fallen, unless it is you or I!"

"Who is to say it is not you and I to Verity?" cried Frederick, doubling his pace.

Lawrence, not being a young man, could not keep up with him and soon the man vanished into the darkness. He knew Frederick carried the stake and hammer and the Holy Water too, so he was armed against the last great vampire of Scar's End.

Liddy listened outside the parlour door for a few more minutes and concluded that Verity was indeed holding her own.

"Love?" cried the vampire, holding his hands over his ears, "It chokes and revolts me...Leave it be, Verity, and join me. Eternal life is sweet and..."

"No, it is not," came the spirited answer, "It is hell on earth, wandering, looking for your next meal, hated by all. However, I love you, Uncle Richard, and God loves you, as does Jesus. He looks to forgive your sins and St Peter waits at the gates of heaven to admit you!"

"No, no, no," screamed Richard, driven into a frenzy by the constant suffocating presence of love.

Liddy ran for the front door, bolted out of it, with just her nightwear and shawl on, and turned up the hill towards Reeve's End, where her eavesdropping, earlier in the day, had confirmed both Frederick and Lawrence were going.

To start with, when he saw the figure of a woman approaching him, Frederick thought it was Verity herself but then, as she drew nearer, he saw the untidy plait and the smaller frame and knew it was Liddy.

"Liddy! Liddy!" he called, "What has happened and where is your mistress? Has Richard got into the house?"

The maid ran up to him, panting profusely, and stopped, one hand on her side.

"Oh, sir...I have such a stitch..."

"But Verity?"

"Yes, yes, the creature has her in the parlour but mistress has the Bible and is reading passages out of it. I came as soon as Jet woke me up!"

"Jet! Is he in danger too?"

"No, no – he is shut in my bedroom but the creature is trying to bite Verity, claiming kith and kin with her for eternity. Oh, hurry, sir, hurry!"

Frederick sped off and Liddy waited for Lawrence, who had caught up and was not so very far behind after all. "What has occurred, Liddy?" he asked the maid and as they ran after Frederick, Liddy told him.

Verity was becoming desperate. She had read the Song of Solomon and now chanted,
"And God so loved the world that he sent his only begotten Son to save it. Yes, to save you too, Uncle Richard. Let God's love save you. Come, end your predation and fly to heaven with a blessing on your lips. I love, love, love you. God loves you too. Feel the love vibration surrounding you..."
"It throttles me," screamed the vampire, crashing about, hardly able to breathe.
"I will wear you down, niece, and you will join me!"
"Never!" cried Verity, "Never whilst there is a grain of love in my body. My love for you, Richard, only grows and grows and grows and grows…."

The vampire had fallen to his knees. The purity of the vibration that Verity emitted was killing him, slowly, it was true, but he could no longer keep his head up.
"Love, love, love," chanted Verity, slowly making a move from her corner but holding out the Bible in front of her, "This book is full of God's love...feel it, Richard," and she touched him on the shoulder with the cover.

Instantly he shot back, writhing around like he had been burnt, uttering curses that made Verity's ears shudder.
"Love, love, love," she carried on, "The love a niece has for her only uncle when she has lost her parents. They send you love too, dear Richard, from the shadowy world of heaven. Love from your sister and brother-in-law. Can you not feel it flooding into your soul?"

Richard was prostrate now and blood ran from his mouth. His eyes flashed green and violet and she knew he was suffering but she had to push on.

"My mother sends you love, as does my father and my brother too, from the world of Spirit. All of them send such love that it embraces you..."

"It strangles me," from Richard, "It kills me...I cannot stand its high vibration and its purity. My soul seeks darkness and depravity. What do I want with love?" He was rolling over and over, hitting his head against the fender and the chairs and leaving blood...fresh, red blood.

"Here is the Song of Love, yet again," cried Verity, turning the pages of the Bible. As she did so she heard the front door bang and she screamed aloud for aid.

"Quick! Quick! He is in here but I am struggling to subdue him!"

The parlour door opened and Frederick was suddenly with her.

"Hold him, Verity...hold him!" he yelled, as Verity pushed her weight against Richard's chest to stop him writhing.

"Love, Richard...love. I bring love," murmured Frederick, soothingly, "Nothing but love anymore. An eternity of love. Love. Love. Love."

He raised the stake as the vampire screamed aloud for mercy and Verity shut her eyes tightly as the jolt of the wood went through her uncle.

One last, loud cry and then a long, deep sigh and suddenly, for the first time, peace entered Richard's life.

Heaven, please be merciful, prayed Verity, and then the room spun, revolved and darkness took her away.

CHAPTER SIXTEEN

Two weeks passed away, and spring further established herself, with flurries of white blossom and nodding daffodils. The moors woke up and deepened their pale winter green, whilst the sheep grazed, unmolested by creatures from the realms of Hades. The village sighed in relief, as day after day went by and no fresh incidents were reported. Both Lawrence and Frederick decided their work here was done.

Richard was buried once again by the wise parson, who had seen things like this before, and Verity was able to put a stone over him, knowing now he would rest in peace. It seemed at times she heard his voice in the house, not angry and mocking her but singing a lullaby as she remembered him when she was a child. His evil had vanished, leaving his soul calm and dreaming of long-forgotten memories before the curse came upon him. There were no more bloodsuckers to perpetrate the dark secret.

Yet all the time buds were bursting and flowers unfolding, Verity said nothing to Frederick about her feelings and finally he despaired.

One day, as April threatened to evict the winds of March, Verity went to her uncle's grave armed with the last of the daffodils from the garden and with a heavy heart, for Liddy had told her that very morning that Frederick was off on the morrow. Apparently the Welsh valleys were once again ringing to the music of vampires and only Frederick could silence them. She sighed. Would she see him before he went? Would he come to say goodbye?

She knelt down and arranged the flowers.
"I wish that we had met under different circumstances," she told Richard. She often came to speak to him; her fear of him had evaporated as soon as the vampire curse left his body and he had been transformed into the uncle of her youth, although try as she might she could not remember him. Yet his features were somewhat familiar to her, for he had her

mother's eyes and the shape of her mouth too. She had even kissed his cold cheek as he lay recumbent in his coffin.

"Grief still surrounds me, Uncle, and guilt too, for my part in your death. But was it really a death? You were Undead and wretched and I could not leave you thus."

A heavy silence fell and then a shadow flitted over the stone and the spring sunshine was interrupted. Verity looked up.

"Indeed we could not," said a voice she at once recognised. Frederick! Her heart missed a beat.

"Richard Arthur Whittle" affirmed the inscription. Verity lowered her head and gave a little sob.

"I am sorry to disturb you, Miss Whittle," Frederick continued.

Miss Whittle! Were they really becoming that formal?

"It is no matter, Frederick," she said, softly now, rising from her knees and dusting her dress and cloak.

"I go tomorrow," he said simply, standing there as though he had been whipped.

"Do you...I mean, must you?" she replied, choosing not to look at him as she could feel her eyes were full of tears.

"But before I go I must know one thing," Frederick pushed on, "How do matters lay between us and it is worth my while coming back?" He had been rehearsing this all night and now it sounded pathetic.

"Worth your while?" queried Verity, playing for time.

"I wonder...that is, I need to know, how I will be received were I to return after Wales is secured," he blundered on.

"Have you not always been received with cordiality?" Verity asked him.

Frederick was silent for a moment and regarded his feet.

"What I said when Alphonso died – it still stands," he whispered, as though to himself.

Verity's hearing was sharp.

"And yet you address me as Miss Whittle, when your heart declares I am your beloved?"

He hung his head a little, feeling confused.

192

"So am I to think of you as Miss Whittle or Verity...my beloved?" he asked at last.

In answer, Verity gave him her hand and suddenly, looked deep into his eyes.

"I am afraid sorrow, grief and guilt has made me cruel and careless," she said, "Forgive me."

"You feel as I do then?" he dared to ask, his feelings making his heart race.

For an answer, she nodded and, arm in arm, they left the world of the sleeping dead to seek the warmth of Verity's parlour.

Three days later it was all arranged and, after the slight delay, Frederick had departed, having left behind a ring on Verity's finger and a licence ready to use for their wedding when he returned. Verity turned the ring now and noticed its powerful shine in the fading firelight, for though it was April the evening was chill.

A betrothed woman, she thought, so soon to be Mrs Pyne. That Frederick would continue his work once they were wed, Verity did not doubt but this time she meant to be with him. They now had a base to which to return, once the curse of the bloodsuckers finally left this country. With Liddy resident as housekeeper, everything would soon fall into place.

Later, she went to bed but sleep evaded her. Despite being happy, she had a feeling all was not well and she could not shake it.

Sitting, musing by the embers of the fire, accompanied by a purring Jet and with Liddy snoring upstairs, a jolt went through her and shook her soul. It was 1.13 in the morning…

Frederick felt Verity's love surrounding him, as he went alone on his first vigil in the Welsh valleys. Lawrence had been struck down with a fever and could not attend.

Assess the situation and then back to marry my beloved, he thought, forgetting the danger of the paths he walked.

193

So, it was Verity's face he saw – in fact, the last picture that flashed before his eyes – as the vampire's fangs pierced his neck and drained the precious lifeblood from him.

TO BE CONTINUED.

Lightning Source UK Ltd.
Milton Keynes UK
UKHW011836010620
364264UK00001B/141